BE
NOT
FAR
FROM
ME

Also by Mindy McGinnis

Heroine

The Female of the Species

This Darkness Mine

A Madness So Discreet

In a Handful of Dust

Not a Drop to Drink

Given to the Sea

Given to the Earth

MINDY McGINNIS

BE
NOT
FAR
FROM
ME

KATHERINE TEGEN BOOKS
An Imprint of HarperCollins Publishers

Katherine Tegen Books is an imprint of HarperCollins Publishers.

Be Not Far from Me
Text copyright © 2020 by Mindy McGinnis
Title page and part opener photograph © 2020 by Getty Images
All rights reserved. Printed in the United States of America.
No part of this book may be used or reproduced in any manner
whatsoever without written permission except in the case of brief
quotations embodied in critical articles and reviews. For information
address HarperCollins Children's Books, a division of HarperCollins
Publishers, 195 Broadway, New York, NY 10007.
www.epicreads.com

Library of Congress Cataloging-in-Publication Data

Names: McGinnis, Mindy, author.
Title: Be not far from me / Mindy McGinnis.
Description: First edition. | New York, NY : Katherine Tegen Books,
  [2020] |
Summary: Lost in the Great Smoky Mountains, rising high school senior
  Ashley Hawkins must fight for survival without any tools, growing in
  awareness that the world is not tame, and neither are people.
Identifiers: LCCN 2019009689 | ISBN 9780062561626 (hardcover)
Subjects: | CYAC: Survival—Fiction. | Great Smoky Mountains (N.C.
  and Tenn.)—Fiction.
Classification: LCC PZ7.M4784747 Be 2020 | DDC [Fic]—dc23 LC
  record available at https://lccn.loc.gov/2019009689

Typography by Erin Fitzsimmons
20 21 22 23 24   PC/LSCH   10 9 8 7 6 5 4 3 2 1
❖
First Edition

For Marlo, Marnie & Ryan
Stride out.

PART ONE

BEFORE

I

WAS

LOST

The world is not tame.

People forget that. The glossy brochures for state parks show nature at its most photogenic, like a senior picture with all the pores airbrushed away. They never feature a coyote muzzle-deep in the belly of a still-living deer, or a chipmunk punctured by an eagle's talons, squirming as it perishes in midair.

If you're quiet in the woods long enough, you'll hear something die. Then it's quiet again. There's no outrage about injustice, or even mourning. One animal's death is another's dinner; that's just the way it is. What remains will go to the earth, yesterday's bones sinking into today's dirt, the only bit of life left where a mouse nibbled, leaving tiny indentations that say there was once something of worth here.

"Gross," Meredith says as I lift a deer skull out from under a layer of dead leaves.

"I thought it was just a drop," I say, giving her a chance to catch her breath at the side of the trail while I check if there's any spinal cord left. Usually the vertebrae are carried off by mice and squirrels, little midnight snacks for them to stash in their burrows.

"A what?" She slips the straps of her backpack off as Kavita catches up to us, holding her jet-black hair in a pile on top of her head, beads of sweat forming on her upper lip.

"A drop," I explain to Meredith. "Bucks lose their antlers every spring, but they're really hard to spot on the forest floor."

I'd been lucky to see this one, mistaking it at first for the bleached white of a dead ash branch. When the entire skull had come up along with the antler I'd barely suppressed my excitement, something that didn't escape notice.

"Why'd we stop?" Kavita asks, dropping her hair so that it falls around her shoulders.

"Ashley's having a *National Geographic* moment," Meredith says.

"Damn straight," I tell her.

"Good thing she knows that shit too," Kavita says,

coming to my defense. "Or else we'd die out here."

That's true enough. Meredith had spotted a mushroom earlier and, assuming that anything that can go on a pizza in the civilized world is safe in the natural one, was about to chow down on a destroying angel. I told her that if I hadn't stopped her in time in about five hours she'd be vomiting and become delirious. But since we're planning on vomiting and being delirious tonight anyway, I don't know that anyone would have even noticed until she started convulsing.

In other words, way too late.

Meredith had sniffed and said, "Then why are they even allowed to grow in a state park, anyway?"

Luckily Kavita was there to defuse the situation and stop me from saying something shitty. I guess being the only person in our school who isn't white has probably taught her a lot about handling confrontation. Me, I just get mad. I'd wanted to tell Meredith we aren't in a state park—we're in a state forest—which means that the trails aren't maintained as well, something she'd complained about the first time we had to straddle a downed tree to stay on the path, and nobody gets to tell poisonous mushrooms where to grow or not grow. It's our job to learn not to eat them.

We live in a place where geography can not only kill you, but also dictates your friends. I don't like many people, and while Meredith has made the cut since kindergarten, it's by a slim margin. She is constantly horrified by the bruises on my legs that blossom under poison ivy rashes; I'm equally turned off by her manicures and the fact that she wing-tipped her eyeliner before coming on this hike. Past our skin, we genuinely like each other. But days like today I have to actually remind myself of that fact.

To be fair, I bet she does too.

"What'cha got?" Kavita asks, motioning toward the skull in my hands.

"A dead animal," Meredith answers for me. "Ash found a dead animal. Please tell me you're not taking that to the party."

Truth is, I'm thinking about it. It's rare to find one in this good of shape, and it's an eight-point, the sharp edges of the antlers still intact. I'm rubbing my thumb along a smooth curve, debating, finally choosing to toss the skull into the leaves. Maybe someone else will find it, hang it on their living room wall or zip-tie it to the grille of their truck.

We head uphill, and I set a pace that will leave Meredith gasping, though Kavita stays steady at my heels. I hold a branch back for her, and she smiles at me as I do, though none of us are talking. We need our energy, need our breath for the long walk to the campsite where the boys and the beers are, somewhere secluded enough that we can get rowdy. It'll be loud later, when we celebrate the beginning of summer vacation, talk about how crazy it is that we'll be seniors next year, the bittersweet tang of something good coming to an end filling our mouths.

But right now it's quiet, and I'm grateful for the silence. In it I can think about what I saw as I turned to go, a perfectly aligned spinal column pressed into the dirt, undisturbed by hungry mouths or digging paws. To be in that kind of condition the deer must not have gone violently, or its bones would have been tossed about by the teeth that took its life. Instead it lay down and died quietly of old age, either dappled by the sun or with soft snowflakes that landed on closing eyes.

It died quiet, under the trees.

I think that's how I'd want to go too.

Hiking—much like drinking—is something that sounds more fun to the uninitiated than it actually is. I'd doubted the intelligence of combining the two ever since Meredith came up with the idea. A party far enough into the Smokies that nobody bothers us might sound like a good time, but both hiking and drinking require enough common sense to get through without seriously injuring yourself, and I've known enough people to prove common sense is anything but common.

I try to remind myself of Meredith's finer points when I spot the electrical cord for a curler trailing out of her pack as she digs for a granola bar. Kavita sees it too and hides a smile. I decide not to tell her that outlets don't grow on trees. I love Meredith. I swear I do. She's just not on my apocalypse-survival team. I, on the other hand, am on everyone's, despite the fact that I keep telling them that in any such scenario I'm striking out on my own because they're deadweight.

"How much longer?" Meredith asks, and I realize she's done me the favor of not asking until now.

I know better than to pull out my phone. There's no more cell service out here than there is the magical electrical current that Meredith is relying on to fix her hair once we're at the campsite. I take a second to get my bearings. The trek we're on is a small leg of the Appalachian Trail, and I've done it enough that a casual glance tells me where I am. I'd love to do the whole AT someday, when I'm older. Or have enough money for a decent kit. Whichever comes first. Probably the older part.

"The guys headed out yesterday," I tell her, eyeing the heavy brush where it's clear someone crashed off the path, probably to take a piss. "They wanted to fish for a bit and set up camp. It's not far, maybe a mile. We'll be able to hear them soon, drunk or sober."

"Drunk, I bet," Kavita says.

"Long as they save some for me," Meredith says, coming to her feet with a rush of energy at the promise of beer. She gives me a smile, and I know I'm forgiven for being . . . myself.

"They'll save some," I assure her, knowing it's true. If not, one of them will probably find a way to brew it on the spot. People like to keep Meredith happy, especially boys. It doesn't matter if her hair looks perfect or not.

She just prefers it that way.

Meredith might not be on my apocalypse-survival team, but I'm probably not on her beauty-pageant roster either, so I guess we've all got our weapons. I might weigh mine before I head out on the trail so that I'm not carrying an ounce more than necessary, and she might keep hers in her bra, but we each get by, in our own way.

"Last leg," I reassure her as she winces, the blister she was nursing not twenty yards into the hike undoubtedly like a hot needle at her heel.

"I'm fine," she says, wiping the sweat from her brow.

And I think maybe I might put her on my apocalypse team as an alternate.

The boys are already lit when we get there, which is more than I can say for the fire. Their priorities definitely went in this order—beer, weed, boobs, fire, tent.

The first two they supplied, we've brought the third, and I'm responsible for everything else. It doesn't look like they went fishing yesterday, or did much of anything other than get high and pass out in sleeping bags under the open sky.

"Ka—vit—a!" Jason lifts a bottle in her direction when we break into the clearing. He's been shouting her name in public since she moved here as a freshman, something Meredith and I have both tried to tell her means he's interested.

Her response is always, "Ja—son!" with the same tone he uses. He's never known what to do with that, so they haven't gone past introductions in two years.

"Hey," Duke says when he spots me, adding an up-nod that must single me out as his girl to the other two guys with them, because they immediately gravitate to Meredith, but they probably would anyway.

She's relieved of the burden of her backpack, given a chair, and manages to initiate the beginnings of the tents going up with a few words and a sly smile. I thank her silently and take a lawn chair next to Duke. At our feet is a pile of sticks they had half-heartedly tossed together, skipping the part where it turns into an actual fire.

"Who're they?" I ask, taking a beer that he pulls from the cooler in between us.

"Couple of brothers. Stephanie's cousins, I guess," he says, pushing back his baseball hat to hold a cold can next to his forehead. "They're visiting, and her mom said to bring them along."

"They cool?" I ask, watching them struggle with a pup tent.

"Seem okay." He shrugs, pausing a second before dropping something on me. "Natalie's coming in later, with Steph."

"Natalie," I repeat, my mouth getting tight. I try to force it back into relaxation.

"That okay?" he asks.

"I don't know, is it?" I shoot back. It doesn't matter how I feel about his ex-girlfriend being here; it's how *he* feels that I'm going to react to.

"Just don't punch her, or anything," Duke says. "I know that's kind of your go-to."

"Once," I tell him, raising a finger. "Once, I punched someone on the basketball court. She'd been over my back all night, and they weren't calling it."

"Probably better your dad said no more contact sports," Duke says, eyeing me over the top of his beer, a sly smile showing his crooked incisor. "Cross-country is a good fit for those legs, anyway."

"Truth," I agree, unable to stop my answering smile. "And a scholarship rolled up in it, so . . . cheers."

"Cheers," he says, touching his can to mine, but we don't say much past that. The fact that my legs are taking me to college and his wallet won't let him follow is something that we both know but haven't talked about yet.

Duke is like this, a lifelong friend that suddenly became something else and knows how to call up that shared history while still making me a little loose in the knees. Meredith could say the same words to me, but she doesn't have that dimple in her left cheek, or the glint in his eyes that's entirely concentrated on me, making me care much less about the imminent arrival of his ex.

"When's she coming?" I ask, leaning back in my chair.

"They weren't even packed when we left, so Tom and Cory asked to come with me and Jason."

"Packed?" I raise my eyebrow, and Duke huffs a small laugh.

"I know, right? Everybody's acting like we're going hard-core or something, not spending one night in the woods. Shit, I bet your pack weighs eight pounds."

"Five," I correct him. "And half that is tampons."

He squeezes his eyes shut against that. "Nice, babe."

"Hey, man, everybody menstruates."

"Not me," he says.

"But I bet I can make you bleed," I tell him, getting a real smile.

"Definitely," he agrees, and reaches out to rub the back of my neck.

It's been like this our whole lives, a little push and pull for sure, but somewhere in between there's a point where we meet, a place no one else is invited. We both grew up in the woods, aware that our friends had other toys like dolls and cars, video games and traveling sports teams our families couldn't afford. We had rocks and sticks, patches of mud and vernal pools where long lines of mosquito larvae hatched.

We discovered this about each other not long after we started dating three months ago, and while it's true we don't always talk a lot, I feel the same way about Duke as I do about the woods. You don't have to be making sounds to communicate, and there's a lot that has passed between us under the stars and leaves that I would never say to anyone else, in words or otherwise.

Duke's mind is following the same track because his hand trails down the edge of my arm to rub the inside of my wrist, the work-worn tips of his fingers leaving a tingling there I'm more than familiar with.

"So you're . . ." He trails off, leaving an edge of disappointment in the air.

"Yeah, I'm bleeding," I tell him. Growing up with just my dad taught me a long time ago that I've got to be blunt about that kind of stuff if I want tampons added to the grocery list.

"Sucks," Duke says. "I kind of wanted to . . ."

"You only *kind of* wanted to?" I tease. "I'm not doing anything with a boy who only *kind of*—"

He cuts me off with a kiss, letting me know that he is more than a little interested in being alone with me, and I'm pretty invested in it too, if it weren't for my current situation, the fact that somebody needs to start the fire, and that we have an audience.

"Ash—ley!" Jason yells at us from his rock perch overlooking the ridge, a fresh beer raised in toast to me. I push Duke back and flip Jason double birds.

"Later," I tell Duke, to which he looks dubious. "There's more than one way to skin a cat," I remind him.

"Girl," he breathes, pulling me close so that I can smell pine resin on him. "You are absolute shit at seduction."

"We're here, bitches!" Stephanie yells two hours later, Natalie trailing behind her.

"You've got the geography part right, anyway," I hear Kavita mutter under her breath. Steph and Kavita have never exactly been close, but in a school as small as ours your friends are limited to people you can stand for small amounts of time. Affection is secondary.

"Hey," Jason says, standing up awkwardly to greet the two girls. He's unsteady on his feet, and I wonder why he made the effort until I get a good look at Natalie. She graduated last year and went off to cosmetology school, leaving Duke in the dust—but adding about fifteen pounds, most of it in her bra. Natalie had always been pretty, but right now she's hot in a way we don't usually see in our corner of the woods, and that extends past the actual limits of the state forest.

Most people here are run-down by thirty, shitty food and cheap beer sagging on their faces and adding to their bellies. The prom kings marry the homecoming queens and age together, telling each other they're still the hottest thing going while checking out the younger generation to see what they've got to offer.

But it's all the same faces in the end, old genes recycled into new skin. We're used to looking at each other and spotting which side of the family your nose came from, or whose eyes you've got. Sometimes a family trait that isn't technically in your tree pops up, and we all politely ignore it.

The weight she's put on hasn't only gone into her chest. Natalie's got curves she didn't have before, and damn if they don't look good on her. She's always had cheekbones you could cut yourself on, but somebody taught her how to use eyeliner, and it's only made her genetic gifts more obvious. Her wide-set eyes always made her look innocent—and while that might have been true at one time, I can tell it's not anymore. She wastes no time giving Duke the once-over, holding his gaze a second longer than she should.

In nature it's the male that does the mating dances, but we somehow got that all backward; it's us girls that learn to do the preening and positioning. And I can tell right off that Natalie's learned more than how to do hair in the year since she left. I can see it in the way she tilts her body the second she spots Duke, a casual dip of her hip and twist of her shoulders, displaying what she's got, bold as daylight.

I don't like it, but I like less that he responds. It's not something I could call him out on without looking like a total bitch, but it's there. He keeps it cool, a nod and a wave that's just two fingers lifted up, nothing more. But something primal inside of him is reaching out in response, and I can feel it, sure as shit, because it's supposed to be directed at me.

And while I've got plenty of self-respect, the pie chart of my personality traits has a huge chunk marked *logical*, and I would never argue that I'm better-looking than Natalie. But there's a large area of that chart marked *hot-tempered*, which is probably why Duke keeps his reaction under control.

"Took your time, coz," one of Stephanie's cousins says. I don't know if it's Tom or Cory, because I didn't bother to sort out who was who when I got here and have put away a few beers since then.

"Doesn't look like we missed much," she shoots back, eyeing a pile of empty beer cans next to the fire that I finally got started after disentangling myself from Duke.

"You all know Natalie, right?" Stephanie says.

"Nat—a—lie!" Jason says, and Kavita promptly punches him in the back of the knee, which sends him sprawling. It's the most interaction they've ever had, so he seems to take it as the compliment it's meant to be.

"Natalie . . . that's perfect," Kavita says to me. On my other side, Meredith remains quiet, her eyes roaming up and down the intruder in her area. My friend is used to being the prettiest girl in the room, and I know what she's doing as she dissects Natalie, trying to assess if her new curves are better than Meredith's, if her skin is smoother now, or her hair glossier since she's got 24/7 salon access. Whatever element Meredith finds herself the winner of, she'll accentuate for the night.

Not that she's got a lot of competition. Tom and Cory have been panting after her all night, but I know

Meredith. She doesn't care if all the boys think she's the better catch or not—she wants Natalie to know it too. And because of that electrical line of attraction still hanging in the air between Duke and Natalie, I feel the same way.

"What's going on?" Stephanie asks, plopping into an empty chair.

"Drinking," Jason says, pulling himself up from the ground, where a mixture of beer and Kavita had landed him.

"That's it?" Steph surveys our faces like it's our duty to supply something better.

"What'd you expect?" Meredith bites back, her words slightly slurred. "A dance party? We're in the woods."

"Which was your idea," Steph answers, cracking a beer despite her disappointment in it being the only entertainment.

"Wow, glad I made it," Natalie says, taking the last seat. "You guys are a good time."

"You almost didn't," either Tom or Cory says, motioning toward the horizon and the dying light there. "Sun goes down on you on this trail, you're done."

"It's marked, dummy," she says, tipping back her beer.

She's right about that much. Though the trail out here is thin, there are white blazes painted on trees every few hundred feet. More than once on the way up I'd had to look for a blaze in the distance, the trail itself lost under new spring growth.

"How you gonna see if there's no sun, genius?" Steph's other cousin shoots back, but she lifts her phone and turns on the flashlight app, right into his eyes.

"And when the battery dies?"

It's my voice, dead solemn. Duke's hand is on my knee, and it flexes just a bit, whether in agreement or warning, I don't know.

"I guess someone would have to come find me." She shrugs, eyes gliding not so stealthily to my boyfriend.

"Vomit," Meredith says.

"Twice," Kavita agrees.

I don't say anything, just open another beer and hope that insipid answer was enough to deter any interest Duke might have had. Then I notice his hand isn't on my leg anymore, and I think maybe a girl's survival skills aren't that big of a deal when all you want to do is screw her anyway.

One of the brothers—I think it's Tom—clears his throat and turns to Kavita. "So where you from?"

"Uh, what?"

If he was looking to break the palpable tension that had spread over the group he picked the wrong person and the worst question. Kavita might not look like the rest of us, but she's as Tennessee as we are, and is damn sick of any implication otherwise.

"Where you from?" he repeats.

"Here," Kavita replies stonily, her beer can audibly crumpling in her hand.

"No, I mean originally."

"She was born in Knoxville, asshole," Jason says, something that takes everyone who knows him by surprise, since it's a complete sentence.

"How'd you know that?" Kavita asks.

"You said, one time," he answers, a blush that the growing shadows can't quite hide spreading through his cheeks.

"Okay, but where are you, like, *from*?" Tom pushes, not picking up what the rest of us are throwing down.

"Jesus Christ, just tell him you're from India," Duke says, and I don't know if it's meant to be insulting to Tom or Kavita. And I don't like that I don't know.

"I'm not," Kavita says stonily.

"I've got to pee," Meredith says, turning to me. "Where's the bathroom?"

"Are you fucking kidding me?" I ask.

Natalie throws a stick onto the fire. "Yep," she says. "Real glad I'm here." And she smiles at Duke.

Which really makes me wish she wasn't.

* * *

More beer doesn't improve things, and a few hours later I'm well aware I need to get away from the fire before I hit someone. I don't even know who it would be. Kavita has lapsed into a moody silence, though she did scoot a few inches closer to Jason, at which point he apparently held his breath and hasn't let it out since. Duke is drinking so much so fast that his glances toward Natalie are getting long enough to verge into staring, and he's not even trying to hide it. Meredith has both Tom and Cory captivated, which leaves me pissed at all three of them for some reason, and Stephanie has settled for making small talk with Natalie, a conversation mostly made up of giggling.

Meredith does a hair flip that I suddenly hate her for, along with the fresh eyeliner she snuck off to reapply before the sun went down. I try to get a grip on the rush of anger, reminding myself that Meredith is not a bad person. Under all that makeup is my friend, and she's played point for me when I'm not in my element. Sophomore year someone nominated me for homecoming attendant and apparently enough people either agreed or thought it would be amusing to see me win that I actually did. I'm more comfortable with a backpack strap across my chest than a sash, so when Meredith helped me pick a dress, perfected my hair and face, and taught me how to walk in heels, it didn't matter to me that it rained on the parade—literally.

I tried to tell everyone on the float that I smelled a storm and they should maybe put a tarp up, but the other girls didn't like the idea of not being able to be seen from all sides. They didn't like looking like drowned rats either, but that was their problem. I was happy enough to be right. Screw my hair.

I grind my teeth and finish the last of my beer, trying not to care that Duke has put some space between us as the night went on. We've never been clingy, and he's always said that his favorite part about me is that I'm not a girly-girl. I don't play with my hair when I talk or try to drink beer in a sexy way. My hair is usually in a ponytail to keep it out of my face, and the beer belongs in my gut in order to serve its purpose, so why be coy?

But all the stuff he's always said he likes me *not* doing seems to look pretty good on Natalie, because all she's done since she got here is toss her mane around and lick aluminum like it's got some kind of nutritional content. It's a show, put on for my boyfriend. And he's watching.

I can be cool and let it slide. Duke likes that I'm low-drama and that I don't freak when I see him checking out another girl, and he returns the favor by not giving me shit when I spend a lot of time at the boys' pole vault during track season. Arms have always been a weakness of mine, and some of those guys have the best triceps I've ever seen. Better even than Duke's, but that doesn't change the fact his arms are my favorite, the only ones that have ever been around me, or touched me, skin to skin.

Out in the dark, something rustles.

It's nothing, my bet is an old limb just fell, and the way Duke stays relaxed next to me I can tell he's thinking the same. But Meredith shoots into the air like somebody set her ass on fire, and Natalie actually makes a move toward Duke, like maybe it's his job to shield her.

"The fuck?" Jason says, alarmed even though he's not sober enough to come to his feet to show it.

"It's nothing," I tell him.

"Nothing, like actually nothing?" Natalie asks. "Or nothing like that time Duke told me it was nothing and a bear ate all our food?"

I do not like thinking about the fact that Duke has taken Natalie camping and they probably only packed one sleeping bag. I like it less that Duke laughs at the memory.

"Oh my God," he says, dimple flashing. "Your face when I unzipped the tent in the morning." He mimics pure shock, and she leans over to smack his arm. I wince at the sound of their flesh meeting.

"It's nothing," I say again. "*Actually* nothing."

"How you know?" Cory—I finally put a face to the name two beers ago—says. And by the way he looks at me, I think maybe if Duke had said it he would've just taken it as gospel. From me, it gets questioned.

"Because I know," I tell him, putting what I'm thinking—*This is my woods, pansy-ass*—into my tone.

His brother doesn't care for that.

"Could be something; could be anything," Tom says. "What'd you say about bears?"

I look to Duke to clarify that what we just heard was not a bear, but catch him holding a hot, smoky stare with Natalie. I'm forcibly reminded that she's who he lost his virginity to.

"Bears," Cory repeats his brother. "Shit, yes, there's bears. That's what got Davey Beet, right?"

"You shut the fuck up."

There's a lot of pissed in my voice, and I don't know how much of it is because of Duke and Natalie, and how much of it is for Davey Beet, but I'm pointing my beer at Cory with two fingers extended, which is pretty much how you start a fight around here.

"Dude, chill," Cory says, hands in the air. "All I said was—"

"She knew him," Duke says. "So shut the fuck up."

"Oh . . ." Cory looks back at me, belated understanding dawning. "Sorry."

I don't respond, aware only that even though Duke backed me up, the distance between us just got wider at the mention of Davey Beet. I get up without saying anything, well aware that if I'm out here much longer somebody is going to get slapped. I've built a pyramid of beer cans beside my chair that topples over as I leave the fire ring, what was inside them now sloshing in my belly. At some point Jason and Kavita have disappeared, something that normally would've amused me, but right now I'm not finding much funny.

I unzip the tent that Duke and I have taken with us on too many trips to count, sometimes forgoing the canvas to have the stars look down on us. Tonight, I'm in it alone, the unnerving cluster of high-pitched laughter following me as I slip down to the ground, head cradled in my arms.

"What's the story there, bro?" I hear Cory ask Duke. "Was she banging him?"

"Really? You're going to ask her *boyfriend* that?" Meredith says, and I know she's staring down Natalie when she says *boyfriend*.

The warm rush of affection I feel is quickly replaced by cold, like someone dropped an ice cube down my throat, when Duke says, "Naw, man. Nothing like that. She just fucking idolizes him."

And then I hear him crush his beer can.

* * *

I don't know if I pass out or what, but there's a fair amount of drool on the side of my face when someone crashes beside me. I wipe it away, hoping I'm not too drunk to reclaim my boyfriend's affections when I roll over to discover it's Stephanie sprawled out beside me.

"Wrong tent," I tell her, but she only groans in response.

"Hey." I give her an elbow, and she slaps at my arm. The next poke gets zero response, so I know she's out cold and there's no point trying to move her. Besides, all the beer that was in my stomach has migrated south, and my bladder is on the verge of bursting.

I slip out of the tent, still drunk as hell but awake enough to zip it behind me so that Stephanie doesn't freeze. It's spring, and away from the fire the night air has a bite to it that she won't welcome. If she can even feel it, that is.

A light breeze blows smoke in my eyes, the fire now down to embers and gray ashes, no one crouching near it for warmth any longer. I hear voices up toward the ridge, a mix of male and female, and assume that the others must have wandered there out from under the canopy to look at the stars.

More than once in my life I've wished that I were a boy, and every one of those times was when I had to take a piss outdoors. There's no graceful way to go about it when you're a girl. And right now I'm not at my most agile, so if I don't want to smell like urine tomorrow I'm going to have to take everything below the waist off.

I start with my shoes, which apparently I passed out wearing, then strip off my socks. Having wet socks is the absolute worst, and if they're soaked in your own piss that makes things about a thousand times more terrible. I've accidentally peed on my socks enough to know, and though Dad could help me with just about everything in life, that particular problem always left him baffled.

I'm far enough from the tents that I don't think anyone is going to be able to hear me, so I strip down to my bare ass and crouch. Sure enough, I fall right over, enough beer still in my veins instead of my bladder to make me unsteady. I push myself back up and do what I came out here for, hoping I really did go far enough away that no one can hear because *damn*.

I'm zipping up my jeans when I hear something that's not natural. Or, actually it is. It's the most natural sound in the world, one you can't hold back no matter how tight you close your throat, the guttural growl of physical pleasure leaking out so that the whole world knows you just had a good time.

I know that noise. And I know exactly who made it

because I'm used to hearing it in my own ear, Duke's body pressed tight to mine. I'm drunk enough that at first it's a dead kind of feeling as I come up on them. Sticks snap under my feet, and I make no attempt to be quiet, since they didn't either.

Duke is pulling his pants up over his ass, bare-chested, and Natalie's shorts are still around her ankles as she sits up, pulling leaves out of her hair.

"What the fuck?" I say.

It's a dumb-ass question. Nobody needs to tell me what was going on, and there aren't any words to take it back or fix it. So Duke and I just stare at each other for a beat, Natalie still finger-combing her hair like it's not her problem.

And I guess it isn't, really. She's not the person I want to punch, not the person who promised me good things and honest words. Not the person who told me we'd get out of here together, load his truck up and just go. That wasn't her; that was him.

"Ashley," Duke says, taking a step toward me.

It's all those good things I'm thinking about when my fist flies. I'm pissed, yeah, but not at this last bad thing. It's all the good stuff I was relying on that just got taken away from me that makes me do it.

I know how to throw a punch. I know where to hit and how hard, my knuckles caving in the bridge of his nose as easily as dry leaves under my boots in the fall. I knock him clean off his feet, the impact jolting up to my elbow as Natalie pulls up her shorts and gets the hell out of there.

Duke just stares up at me, dark blood dripping onto his chest in twin rivers, his hands cupped over his broken nose. He doesn't yell though. Doesn't argue or call me a crazy bitch or anything I've heard other guys do when their girl gets up in their face about something they totally deserve to be dressed down for. Duke doesn't do those things, because he's taken beatings for stuff in his life that weren't his fault, letting his dad's fists rain down on him for leaving the trash cans on the curb even though it was his little brother that did it.

This is on him, and he knows it. So he took his beating, and now he's just sitting there waiting for the rest, maybe a kick to the ribs or a ball-crushing from the arch of my foot. But I don't have it in me anymore. All the rage pulsed out in that one savage arc that left the smell of blood in the air, tinged with the scent of sex soaking into the forest floor. It's him I smell around me, every bodily fluid he's got filling my nose as he starts crying tears to match mine, both of us hitching big sobs that can't be put back inside.

"Ash . . ." He reaches for me, slow, like I'm an animal in one of his live traps that might bite. And that's just what I am and exactly where I'll be if I stay here one more second, because I can't look at this boy who I hurt in return for hurting me. I can't hear my name on his lips without loving it, even though another girl's mouth was just crushed underneath them.

If I stay, he'll stand up and I'll go to him, fitting my head into that spot under his chin where I fit so perfectly. And, yeah, I'll get blood on my face if I do that right now, but he'll forgive me and I'll do the same for him and I won't ever have the courage to walk away because he's the only boy I ever had for my own.

So I do what any scared animal does. I run.

I have no idea which direction I'm pointed or how far I'm going. All that's important right now is that I go fast, away from Duke and the smell of him and her. I'm still barefoot, because I never bothered putting my shoes back on after hearing that low hum of satisfaction. Sticks are breaking under my feet, a good sharp jab going into the arch and stealing my breath, but not enough to make me stop crashing through the brush and tearing like a crazy woman down a ridge and back up another one.

It's a good, hard fall that finally gets me. My bare toes jam underneath a boulder sticking out of the hillside, and the whole thing shifts. I throw myself to the side, pinned foot crushed as the boulder rolls. There's a moment when my foot resists but then gives under the superior weight of the rock. It's like stepping on a big spider or smacking a fat winter fly. There's a moment of resistance and then . . . something gives. Except it's no bug that just got crushed, but my own bones. The rock tears downhill, taking out saplings as it goes, but I'm stopped for good as the pain takes hold, puncturing the drunkenness.

I try to stand but pitch forward instead, grabbing for a tree so that I don't roll downhill along with the rock. I hit the ground again, a knotty root getting me right in the stomach so that I'm lying facedown in a cloud of my own stale breath, shoeless.

"Fuck," I manage to say, rolling over so that I can get a good lungful of air. The first one hurts, like it always does after a good punch to the gut. But I pull it in anyway, forcing everything in there to open up and keep going.

The moon stares down at me from an angle that says daylight's a long way off. I don't know how far I ran or which way the camp is. Yelling for my friends and Duke is going to bring a lot of questions about why I took off and what happened to his nose, and where had he and Natalie gone off to in the first place, and why.

I don't feel like answering those questions right now, maybe not ever, so I pull myself the rest of the way up the ridge and take a look at my foot. It's smashed to shit, my little toe nearly flat and the two next to it scraped wide-open. It's dark, and I'm too drunk to feel much, but I know I'll be hurting in the morning. It's still bleeding freely, so I pull my shirt off and wrap it around my foot, knowing full well it needs cleaning, but I'm in no shape to do it.

The adrenaline that sent me into a mad dash has faded, and the beer in my bloodstream is reasserting itself, fading the edges of my vision and telling me to lie back down, fast. There's a stick in my back, and the wind blows a leaf right into my cleavage, frayed edges crackling against my skin as I roll onto my side, exhaustion claiming me. I'll find everyone in the morning, face Duke and their questions and Natalie's snide smiles. Right now all I've got is self-pity and a throbbing pain in my foot, so I let both take me down into unconsciousness.

Because it's so much better than being aware right now.

PART TWO

WHEN
I
WAS
LOST

DAY ONE

When I wake up I know two things.

One is that it's nearly noon and somebody should've come looking for me by now. And the other is that I have really fucked up my foot. In the moonlight all I could make out was the damage done to my toes, but once I unwrap my shirt there's a lot more on display, and none of it should be visible.

The human foot is a complicated thing, and I know a lot about it after putting hundreds of miles of trail underneath mine. When you hike as much as I do you learn that small parts you didn't know you had can hurt until it seems like it's the only bit of you to feel anything at all. There are twenty-six bones in my foot, and right now I can see a handful of them, plain as day, as well as a tendon with a tear that is going to send me into a world of pain as soon as I try to stand up.

But I've got to, because the sun is high, and my head is pounding, my lips cracked and begging for a drink. Water is my first priority, and I'm lucky enough to remember splashing through a stream last night before keeling over. I pull myself to the edge of the ridge and spot it, although using the word *stream* would be an exaggeration.

It's a trickle of water, runoff from places higher than this one, going in search of something lower. Everything it touches as it heads downward is in there; animal shit and rotting plants, all kinds of things that I don't want in me but don't have much choice about right now. If I had my pack, I could drop a purification tablet into my canteen, but I don't even have my canteen. All I've got is my mouth and my hands, and I guess it's enough because a few minutes later I'm not thirsty anymore. I'm worried about my foot and if I just ingested any bacteria, but mostly the basic part of me needed a drink, so I went and got one.

My next challenge is going to be standing up.

I know it's going to hurt, know that fresh blood is going to gush and agony will rush up my leg and take over my head in a black wave. But knowing doesn't make

it any easier, and a noise comes out of me no sane person can make, as I lean against a tree for support and
force myself to breathe in deep breaths until the spots
in my vision start to fade.

So I'm up. Now I've got to walk.

My immediate thought is *Fuck that*. But my other
option is to yell for help, and to be honest I'd rather
pass out four or five times on the way back to the campsite than admit that I need it. It's deep inside me, a
gene come down from my momma that drove her to
do everything alone—even that last thing, which was
leaving. That little bit of DNA is mixed in with my
dad's inability to say he was wrong about something,
an explosive mix that blew their marriage to bits when
I was just a kid.

Put those things together inside of one person
instead of facing off and what you get is me. I'm a living
example of the old saying "If you want something done
right, do it yourself," because I sure as hell am never
wrong and other people just get in my way. Even when
my foot is flayed open and I'm alone in the woods, I am
not calling for help. I'll drag myself back to camp on my
elbows before I admit I can't do this on my own.

Thing is, I'm not so sure which way camp is. I was
hurting in more ways than one when I ran last night.

Drunk, hysterical, injured. I don't know how far I went or what direction I was pointing, which is an issue. It's like a math equation—there can only be so many unknown variables before it becomes an unsolvable problem. I can find north easy enough, but I don't know which way the camp is.

I lean forward, grabbing for the next tree that can hold me and taking a hop, bad foot in the air. The pain is enormous, but I grit my teeth and aim for the next tree until I can scan the far ridge closely.

I've never been much of a hunter, but Dad taught me to track so that I'd know what was in the woods with me. Looking for the passage of something as big as an insane teenage girl should be easy, I think, as I look for signs I made last night. There's a decent furrow where it looks like I went down on my shoulder and slid a good ways toward the stream, and a break in the bracken at the top where I busted through.

Good enough. I take a deep breath, bracing myself for the climb—which is nearly impossible when all I can do is hop. I fall twice, misjudging the reach of my arm and ending up with a face full of leaves, and once nearly losing an eye on a downed limb. Even then I won't yell for my friends; instead I say *Goddammit* under my breath and get back up. I figure God can hear me, at least, and should know how I feel about the situation.

By the time I reach the top my foot feels like a lead weight at the end of my leg, and my knee hurts from keeping it bent. There's sweat running down my face and pooling in my bra, but goose bumps popping underneath it when I pass into the shade. It's not warm and not cold right now. It's the perfect temperature to make you unhappy both ways.

But it's the least of my problems once I reach the top.

I bitch all the time about people who don't know how to walk in the woods, the ones that break branches and kick up noise, turning over rotting wood with one step and crushing new growth with the next. I don't want to hike with them, for sure, but I wish in this moment that I was one of them.

Apparently even when I'm a drunk crazy woman I don't leave a trail.

I swear and slide to the ground, leaning back against a tree for support. I stretch out my knee and take a good look at my foot, trying not to get freaked about the fact that my tendon is taking a good look back at me. It's not bleeding so much anymore, but it's starting to swell from hanging at the end of my leg like a pendulum. I take my shirt back off and tie it tight around my foot, ignoring the throb of pain from my own pulse as I do.

I blow out everything I've got in one breath, thinking hard. I couldn't have gone far, but time is slippery when you're drunk. Conversations that you drift in and out of seem to last for hours instead of only minutes. So I guess it's possible I ran longer than I think, which is not good. A wave of panic crests in my gut, pushing its way up into my throat and threatening to squeeze tears out of my eyes.

I will not cry.

For one thing I'm not lost, so it would be stupid. For another—whether I'm lost or not—it'll dehydrate me. And last, suppose Duke or Kavita or Meredith comes up on me while I'm sitting twenty yards from the camp in my bra and crying.

"Nope," I say to myself at the thought. "Not happening."

I. Am. Fine.

So I get up, and I look for blazes.

Natalie—bless her dirty little soul—was right about the blazes she mentioned last night. They're useless at night, but in the daylight they should stand out against the trees. I'm off-trail, no doubt, but I can't be too far off. I steady myself and look around, straining my eyes as far as I can see, ignoring the quick dash of a squirrel and knock of a woodpecker. All I want in the world right now is a blob of white paint.

I don't see one.

"Well, shit," I say.

I have options.

I can try to find my shoes. Even the thought of putting my crushed toes into them makes me flinch, but I can at least put my right one on and make better time back to the road . . . once I find the trail. And if I can find my shoes then surely—*surely*—I can find the campsite. I didn't wander too far just to take a piss, and the white of my socks should show up like a beacon in all this brown and green.

It's true. I should be able to spot them right away, and that simple fact both comforts and terrifies me. Because finding them should be easy . . . unless I ran so far away last night that I can't see a flash of bleached white in the middle of a gray afternoon in the woods.

"It's okay," I say. "You're fine."

I don't know why I'm talking, but the words break up the thoughts that were starting to form. If I can't find the campsite, then picking up the trail is going to be . . .

"It's not impossible," I say, biting down on the words, wanting them to feel more substantial.

Around me, the woods have fallen quiet, the unfamiliar echo of my voice sending everything into a standstill, tiny ears perked. Mine do too, my mouth closing. There's a questioning chirp from a robin, the answering knock of a woodpecker, and then a squirrel climbs a tree about forty yards away, circling it as he ascends. He's unconcerned, tail big and bushy, not in any kind of hurry.

And that means nothing good for me. If I'm anywhere near my friends, the woods would be quiet, their morning-after grumblings and good-natured teasing carrying into the trees, hushing the birds and keeping every animal on the alert. There's nothing like that here. As soon as I went silent, the woods around me came to life, carrying on as if there was no predator in the area.

Because there's not.

Which means I'm alone.

"Shit," I say. "Shit, shit, shit."

The squirrel peeks out at me from between branches, surprised. He chatters to let everyone else know there's a problem and keeps an eye on me, well aware I can't do anything to him from the ground. And I can't. I couldn't do anything to anybody other than freak out on them right now. It pisses me off, so I grab a handful of dead leaves and toss them in his direction, which only gets me another earful from him and dirt in my hair as it falls back on me. The squirrel adds his last thought, then pops into his nest.

"Dick," I mutter.

It comes out funny because I'm about to cry, my

mouth all twisted up. It sounds a little like my boy-friend's name, actually. But I'll die right here with my shirt on my foot and my back against a tree before I yell for him. Somebody else though . . . I might have to admit that calling for help is where I'm at.

Except that word is ugly to me, like how Meredith won't say *God* in front of *dammit*. So it's her I'm thinking about when I yell, and her name bounces back at me off the trees.

"Meredith!"

It kills the woods dead, everything hearing the edge in my voice, sending my fear right into them. Except that damn squirrel. His head comes up out of his nest like he's afraid he might miss something. I try again, taking a deep breath right down to the bottom of my lungs and screaming my friend's name so loud that it hurts in my foot.

"MEREDITH!"

Nothing. I picture her still wiped out in a tent, hands flat under her cheek the way she always sleeps, like one of those stupid baby angels in a painting. I don't know if I'm thinking about it that way because I want so badly for them to still be here, or if I just like the idea of someone else being warm.

Because I'm not. The breeze has picked up, sending the mottled shade around me into a kaleidoscope as the canopy shakes. With it comes a smell I usually love, but not right now. Rain.

"KAVITA!"

I tell myself that her name is sharper, will travel farther. Nobody answers.

"DUKE!"

It tears out of me before I said it could, desperation in my voice that's got everything to do with being alone, not only just right here, right now. But there's no calling back, no voice to answer me. I think of Jason, yelling girls' names all the time, and I think this could have been his moment, but he's not here for it.

"STEPHANIE!"

It's my last shot, and it takes all the breath I've got left, three syllables projecting in a voice that the drama teacher kept begging me to put on the stage ever since all the mics got blown out in a power surge. There's no response. I can't remember the brothers' names, which leaves Natalie.

I consider it for a second, my mouth hanging open in indecision.

"Fuck that," I say instead.

There's no point, because there's no one here. They probably woke up, hungover and grumpy, maybe not even noticing I was gone until they took down the tents, expecting me to be inside of one. I imagine Duke keeping his head low, trying to hide his nose, Natalie breezily ignoring any questions about when she saw me last.

Maybe they would come clean. Explain that I'd come across them in the woods, *talking*. I'm sure that's all they would admit to, leaving out that neither of them was wearing pants. Duke wouldn't be able to cover his nose forever, and everyone would know I broke it, and they'd probably guess why.

And if I was mad enough to do that, I was probably done with the whole thing, and every one of them, too. I probably left. I bet they imagined a pissed-off Ashley, headed back to the road and hiking into town, getting a ride home from my uncle Chuck at the gas station. I can hardly blame them for thinking it, since that's exactly what I *should* have done—and would have if I hadn't been so drunk.

Somebody would've grabbed my pack, doing me a favor.

With that thought comes the first grumble of my stomach.

Things change from *going to rain*, to *definitely raining* pretty quick. The fast pattering of drops deflected by leaves switches into a downpour without much warning. I've got nothing for cover, and no time to make any shelter. I remember seeing a decent-size spruce tree back the way I came, so I lurch onto my good foot and try a few hops, grabbing for anything to keep me upright as I go. I'm drenched when I find the spruce again, water running down my nose right into my mouth and more following the path of my spine down to my underwear.

I'm wet in every place I've got, so it doesn't matter a lot when I drop to the ground and slide under the lowest boughs of the tree, knocking loose the droplets clinging to each needle. It doesn't make me any wetter, but it doesn't make me any warmer either. The rain sitting on my skin might be stealing my body heat, but the drops that land fresh are cold and not finding a lot of warmth left to take. I push with my good foot and drag with my elbows until I'm up against the trunk, the tree shielding me not from everything but from a lot of it.

"Okay," I say to myself, voice barely rising above the din of the storm. "Where do I stand?"

I immediately start laughing, because I can't even *stand.* My foot hurts so damn bad it's all I can think about, my brain constantly processing pain signals and not allowing for much else. But I've got to, because I can either lie under this tree and think about how shitty I feel, or I can do something about it.

Doing something is what I'm good at, Dad always says so, and that I got it from Mom. He'll lean on a shovel in the yard and look at a tree that needs to go in the ground for twenty minutes, talking out the different ways to go about digging a hole unless I kick the shovel out from under him and just start digging it.

At this moment I'm in a hole for sure, and one I dug myself.

I have nothing, and I'm injured. That's the first thing that comes when I decide to take stock. It's a shit answer, and one sure to send me into another panic if I let it. So I stare it down and call it wrong.

I have a shirt, a bra, and underwear. I have a pair of jeans—thank God I didn't change into the cute little shorts Meredith insisted I pack. Right now my shirt is on my foot, something that needs to be rectified. Putting it back on soaking wet is only going to chill me further, but once this rain stops I'll need to dry my clothes. I also need to keep my wound clean, which is my first problem.

I unwrap the shirt gingerly, wincing as the last few inches come away and the big flap of skin lifts up with it. The only thing holding my foot together *is* my foot, the bones a bright, shining white in a sea of pink. I'm definitely swollen, but everything looks reasonably clean enough, and I'm not bleeding anymore.

Well, at least from there, anyway.

Shit.

I prop my foot up on a branch and lie back on the carpet of needles beneath me, surprisingly soft on the bare skin of my back. I blow out a long breath, thinking about all the things in my pack. Food. Dry clothes. Tampons.

Menstruating in the woods is not a big deal, usually. Duke used to make a lot of stupid jokes about bears (I laughed because I thought I was supposed to), but it's no different than anything else. The old question "Does a bear shit in the woods?" can easily be changed into "Does a woman menstruate in the woods?"

The answer is the same. And just like the bear, nobody ever witnesses it because it's really not that remarkable. Unless you're lost and verging on a toxic-shock-syndrome situation sometime in the near future. I've got enough problems as it is. I decide I'd rather wander through the forest for the next week smelling like an uncooked roast than have a headline read, LOCAL GIRL, 17, KILLED BY TAMPON.

I snort out a laugh, surprising myself.

I should be a lot of things right now. Scared. Sad. Angry, even. But apparently I'm amused by my situation.

"Get a grip, Hawkins," I say, and go back to listing my assets.

Shirt. Bra. Jeans. Underwear.

That's it. But I can work with that.

I turn my tee inside out, inspecting the seams of the sleeves. Most of my clothes have a few years' wear on them, and this one is no different. It's an old softball jersey from a co-ed summer team that I played on with Dad's bar buddies. They put me on the roster as an alternate until a pregnancy and a breakup wiped some of the ladies off the list. I showed up with my bat and told them I played infield or I didn't play.

They laughed in a good-natured way, told me of course I'd be in the dirt. They wouldn't think of putting Vern's daughter anywhere else. Dad had let his buddies give me a hard time, knowing I'd take care of it myself. So I turned a double play and ran down a tag on a guy who'd been staring at my ass from the other dugout, leaving him with no more catcalls in his mouth, just a bunch of grit in his teeth from where he dove for second. But I beat him there.

I wore this shirt two more seasons, until injuries, new babies, and at least one case of addiction left us with a sad lineup that couldn't take a trophy in a seniors' league. We faded out, but I kept the shirt, and now I'm eyeing a loose string I think I can get at with my teeth. It comes away easy enough, so I start picking with my fingers, careful not to break what's already pulled free.

I get pretty far before I lose too much light. The storm's rolling in and stealing hours of daylight, bringing in the dark before the sun is actually gone. I've got a length of loose thread about as long as my hand, and I might be able to get the sleeve off with a good yank. I'd be smarter to wait until morning, take the time to pull each tedious stitch so that I'd have a bandage for my toes and some string. But I can't do that.

I can't do that, because I'm Ashley Hawkins, and I have not accomplished a damn thing today except panic, cry some, and bleed all over myself in more places than one. That is not acceptable, and I will not sleep with no shirt on and nothing covering an open wound in my foot.

"Nope," I reassert, yanking the sleeve free.

It comes off easier than I expected, and my hand hits the tree trunk hard enough to bring a sting that burns past the cold that's soaked down to my bones. It's like stubbing your toe, there's a moment where it doesn't quite hurt *yet* and then . . .

"Fuuuuuccccccckkkkk," I say, cradling my hand to my wet stomach and rocking over it like it's a baby I'm trying to put to sleep.

But I got what I wanted.

I slip the sleeve over my injured foot, the name of our team—Designated Drinkers—facing up. It's not much, but it'll keep dirt out. I squeeze as much water as I can out of what's left of my shirt and slip it on. It's cold against my skin, and every inch of me shies away from it. But I've got nothing else, and it doesn't look like it's going to stop raining any time soon. I turn on my side, curl into a ball, and, amazingly, fall asleep.

DAY TWO

I wake up to pain.

My foot throbs with each push of my heart, which I can't imagine means anything good. And I'm freezing. *No.* I correct myself, knowing that once I start using words like that I might have to learn a hard lesson about the difference between being cold and actually dying from it. That's what freezing is. And I'm not dead.

"Nope," I agree with myself.

A few winters ago we had what the TV weatherman called a polar vortex. It was so cold you had to bring your car battery indoors with you if you wanted to go anywhere in the morning, and you didn't go outside unless it was worth maybe not coming back in. We didn't have school for a week, and of course I'd managed to drop my

phone in the toilet, so I was cut off from Meredith and
Kavita and Duke sure as if I'd died anyway.

But my dad didn't raise any pansies, so when the garbage can got full I figured it wasn't so cold that a person
couldn't burn trash. Our cupboards were low, and we'd
been eating tuna for two days, so the trash can had a
funk about it that filled up the whole trailer. I was done
with smelling it, done with staying inside, and done
with people on TV telling me I couldn't go outside. So
I bundled up same as I would in any cold, grabbed some
matches, and went out to the burn barrel.

The wind cut through my clothes like I might as well
have been naked, and by the time I reached the barrel
I knew I'd made a bad decision, but I was already out
there and I wasn't leaving a garbage bag with rotting
tuna scraps in the yard. We might be poor, but we aren't
trash. The first match I tried to strike blew out. My
fingers were already numb when I went for the second
one, fumbling and stupid. I dropped it.

My legs were aching when I pulled the third, a steady
thrum that had started at my feet and crawled to my
knees, already stiff and locked against the wind. I realized too late what was happening and turned back to
the trailer only to fall flat on my face into the snow.
My legs were useless, dead sticks attached to a living
body that wasn't going to be that much longer if I

didn't figure some shit out, fast.

I managed to get back up, forcing my feet—so heavy, so awkward—to move by sheer willpower. I made it about ten yards before red filled my vision and I went down again, a little *oof* coming out of my mouth that blew up snow in a tiny blizzard in front of my face.

No mattress had ever been as comfortable as that snow, and I had never been as tired in my life as I had been in that moment. I've heard that drowning people hear singing, and then have a moment of calm before the end. I don't know if it's the same for everyone that's almost frozen, but I saw cans of tomato soup.

Meredith laughed when I told her that, but Kavita got quiet and looked at me hard.

"Why did you see soup?" she asked, her intensity drawing Meredith's attention away from trying out new braids in her hair.

"I don't know." I had shrugged, body still sore from the experience. "I guess maybe I knew I wasn't going to make it, and my brain wanted to give me a good thought, let me think of something warm to make me feel better as I went out."

Tomato soup was the best it could come up with, one nice memory I still have of my momma before she split. She wasn't much of a cook, but you really can't screw up tomato soup. So that was a winter-weather meal at our house, complete with grilled cheese that Dad usually did because Momma's tended to be burned.

Dad spotted me lying in the side yard, seeing lines of soup cans that weren't there. He hauled my ass inside and put me in front of the kerosene heater until I unfolded my limbs, each one of them still shaky and weak. We couldn't really afford the copay on our insurance unless one of us was bleeding out, so he just did what made the most sense to him for someone with hypothermia— kept me warm and fed me chicken broth. I slept forever once I found the couch, maybe could have even faded on out if Dad hadn't kept waking me up to ask me if I was alive.

I was alive then. I'm alive now.

So I know I'm not freezing out here under this tree, because I sure as hell haven't seen any tomato soup, and if I did, you can be damn sure I'd have eaten it already.

I'm not starving either, that's the other thing. I'm hungry, which means I'm fine. I've gone a day or two without food in my life, always playing up like I'm on a diet or something when I show up to lunch without anything to eat. Meredith would make a joke, say she's getting chubby anyway and slip me half her sandwich. I'd try not to eat it in three bites, really focus on not tearing into bologna and cheese like it was the best thing that ever happened to me.

But sometimes it would be because Dad wasn't getting any overtime.

Meredith might be dumb, but she's not stupid—there's a difference. She was always watching, and if I went a couple of days on one of my so-called diets she'd have me over for the weekend and order in everything, from pizza to Chinese to the one questionable Thai place that's totally run by a white guy.

"So I'm not starving," I say aloud, breaking up the memory of Meredith and piles of food. Because while I'm grateful to her and always will be, thinking of that food and not having it in front of me hurts.

No, I'm not freezing and I'm not starving, and I know both these things are true because I'm in pain.

When you can't feel anything is when you need to worry.

My foot doesn't look any better in sunlight.

The day snuck up slow, and I watched it come, along with a momma raccoon leading her babies back to their den, the smallest one stopping to pick up things with its little hands. It turned over a few sticks just to see what was under them, then its momma came back for it, rounded it up with the brothers and sisters, and the little family filed out of my sight.

Those things are so cute you've got to remind yourself that they're actually nasty little bastards that'll tear kittens into pieces while they're still alive just to get to the tasty bits. It's a good reminder that my own tasty bits are hanging out of my foot, so I crawl out from under the spruce once daylight is full-on.

My foot is wrinkly from having a wet sleeve wrapped around it all night, the skin pulling back from the wound even further. I have to tug on the sleeve harder to take it off than I did to put it on, so I must be swelling. Everything looks clean, but I know by the time I can see an infection, it'll already be too late.

The sun gets high enough that I can feel warmth from its rays, so I strip down, taking everything off. I throw my clothes over branches and let the breeze do the rest while I sit, hunched and naked on a downed tree.

My skin is mottled, red and white, the sun not doing enough against the chill of the wind. I look like marble, blood and flesh instead of rock and mineral, and I wonder if anyone were to come along if I'd yell for help or ask them to admire me for a minute first.

It's funny, and I laugh again, wondering if this is part of the process of losing it, which is something I don't get to do.

I don't get to, because I thought about my situation

while I lay in the moonlight under the tree and realized not only did I get left behind but also no one's coming to look for me either.

Dad's pulling a double shift and then crashing at a buddy's, probably pulling in more pay if he can, and headed right back to the factory after grabbing a few hours of sleep. I can assume my friends thought I headed for home, and somebody picked up my pack for me, my phone buried deep underneath layers of clean underwear and more than likely dead by now.

Whoever took my stuff might drive it over to the house and leave it there for me, not thinking anything of the fact that I'm not home. If Dad's there—and awake—there might be a conversation where two and two gets put together, but I can't count on that. To be honest, Duke's probably the one who would've thought to grab my gear, and I doubt he's in any hurry to come face-to-face with me or anyone I'm vaguely related to any time soon.

I give it three days, maybe more, before connections are made and everyone realizes I'm still in the woods.

I look at my foot, turning it different ways in the morning light.

I don't think I have that much time.

* * *

On a good day I can put in eight miles on the trail.

I assume I will not be having a good day, but I do know not having shoes isn't the setback it seems. More than once I've been on trails with people who put a lot of money into serious boots, not realizing that their leg has the job of lifting that extra two pounds on each foot with every step. And that adds up, taking them down by midday and draining them empty by nightfall—if they don't give up and turn around.

I'll take my shoes off when I'm hiking if the trail is clear, loving the freedom of dirt in between my toes. So my one good foot being bare isn't too much of an issue. It's the other one I need to come up with a solution for.

I tear back into my shirt once it's dry, biting a tiny, puckered hole with my canines that I widen with my fingertip, then I push my whole finger through. I rip off a section from the bottom as wide as my hand, and loop one end over my right arm and let the other end dangle near my ass. It's not easy, but I get my bad foot up and hook it through the other end, looking back over my shoulder and inching the makeshift sling down to my ankle.

It's not bad. My heel is practically touching my butt, and my knee will be screaming in a few hours, but the wound is out of the dirt and I don't have to waste a bunch of energy holding my leg up.

The next thing I need is a goal. When my famil-iarity with punching got me kicked off the basketball team and Dad suggested the nonconfrontational sport of cross-country, I was less than enthused. I wanted to be in it, fighting for something, swinging elbows while I grappled for the ball.

My attitude must have been obvious on the first day of practice, 'cause Coach pulled me aside and told me I looked like I wanted to fight somebody. I told him maybe I did, and what the hell kind of competition is there in running?

"Competition?" Coach had asked, pushing his hat back off his forehead. "Okay, tell you what, smart-ass. Give me three miles, then come back and see what kind of fight you got left in you."

I had shit left, but I took his point. My opponent was myself, the very deep pain that welled within me from mile one the only thing I had to overcome to keep going. I couldn't run the whole three, puked twice, and got back to Coach with swollen feet and a blister the size of my ass on one heel.

He'd pulled me up off the ground, settled my palms on top of my head so I could take deeper breaths, and said, "Tomorrow, try harder."

Coach saw me for who I was right from the beginning—someone who wasn't going to back down from that kind of an insult. So I came back the next day and tried harder, and the next, pushing past pain to the runner's wall, where the only things that exists are your feet, the ground, and a point in the distance.

Which is exactly what I need right now. A point in the distance.

"Today you're going to walk two miles in one direction," I say aloud, making it official. There is no response, not even that one chatty squirrel. Just the wind, taking my words.

I didn't make a fire last night, but I've got to leave something behind so that if anyone is looking for me, they'll know I was here, and where I went after. I gather enough stones to form an arrow, pointing the direction I'll be headed once I set out.

The first bit of luck to find me comes in the form of a walking stick I spot nearby, with a notch at just the height for my armpit. It's not a perfect crutch, but perfection is pretty far from reach, since I haven't eaten in twenty-four hours and am currently a free bleeder.

I tuck it under my arm, leaning gingerly forward to see if it'll support my weight. It does, and I take first one hop, then another. I'm hunched like an old woman and swearing like an old man, but I'm moving.

"All right, Ashley Hawkins," I say, squaring my shoulders as best I can while using a crutch. "Go be a badass." And with that, I inch forward.

Water will always follow the path of least resistance, something I don't have the luxury of doing. It will split around rocks, make turns to avoid tree roots, then head back the other way like maybe it left the stove on at home. And while this makes for a lovely postcard, it is a bitch of a thing when you need to head in one direction but stay hydrated at the same time.

Dad has always been proud of the fact that I know which way I'm pointed, no matter where we go. He says people these days are so stupid they couldn't find north if their nose was magnetized, and from what I've seen on the trails, this is somewhat true. My innate sense of direction has always been a point of pride for me, and more than once I've had to correct Duke about which path to take in order to reach where we were headed.

Granted, it's easy to lose your bearings. Most make the excuse it's because everything looks the same in the woods, but that's like saying we're all pink on the inside. If you pay attention, there's as much difference between one tree and the next as there is in people. I know I won't end up walking in circles for these reasons—I know which way I'm pointing, and I pay attention to everything I pass.

What can happen though—and will—is that no matter how hard I try to walk in a straight line west—which should be the shortest route out of here—I'm going to pull to the south because I'm leaning that way due to my injury. And it's impossible to walk in a straight line in the woods anyway, for the same reason blue lines of water on maps are curvy messes.

A downed tree, a slippery ledge, a scree that could go out from under me with no warning. If I see these things I'll avoid them, which means going off one way or another, never quite sticking to true west. I know how to make a shadow stick—a nifty trick involving the morning sun and a decent-size stick jammed in the ground sundial-style. You mark the end of the shadow, wait a bit, then mark where the shadow has moved to and bisect those two lines, and your new line is pointing east-west. I can course correct every morning if I need to, but a shadow stick only works if the sun is out, and I'll be adding miles every time I go around any obstacle that points me anywhere other than west. Miles mean time, and that's something I don't have.

I also don't have water, something that's more of a problem than I want to admit. It's there, for sure, in all the little ravines and low places where the water goes. I know better than to touch still water—anything placid can get warm, cooking all kinds of bacteria and who knows what else in its depths. Moving water I will drink, and one of those would lead me to a stream, and I could follow that to something bigger, which would eventually take me to civilization.

If I had food and wasn't hurt it might be the smart choice. But those little trickles of water will take their time getting to where they're going, leading me through switchbacks and big, looping curves that will drain all my energy.

It's what Dad would call the scenic route, and I don't have time to appreciate nature when it's trying to kill me. The shortest distance between two points is a straight line, so I'm going to make one as best I can and find water along the way.

It's late spring so it shouldn't be too much of a problem. The rain that I was cursing last night will be my saving grace today, so I hobble down to running water when my path crosses with it, but I don't follow the siren call of its bubbling voice.

I've been moving for about three hours when I decide it's time to go down to the water I can hear on the other side of the ridge I'm climbing. It's slow moving, my hopping forward and grabbing for trees while trying not to lose the walking stick. I go down twice, once onto my stomach, knocking out my wind and sending the bitter taste of bile into the back of my mouth.

The second time I go backward, arms wheeling on both sides of me as I fall. I let out a scream that's nothing compared to what comes out when I land, flattening my foot between my ass and the ground. It's a primitive sound, all rage and pain, one that stills the forest around me. Everything knows that something big just got hurt, and like most small animals, they know their best bet is to keep quiet and lie low.

There's a wetness spreading on my rear end, and it's not cold groundwater. It's warm, and the full, heavy scent of blood reaches me a moment later.

"Shit," I say up to the sky, as black circles start forming in my vision. I can't pass out, so instead I pick one and name the shapes it becomes as it travels.

Fish.

Bear.

Buzzard.

Screw that. I'll call it an eagle.

I can't look at my foot, not yet. For one thing I'm pretty sure my head isn't ready for me to sit up. For another, the silence has swallowed me, the self-protective quiet of the woods reminding me of Duke's house.

My house was more welcoming, but also smaller, and the two of us couldn't hope for a lick of privacy even if

Dad was sleeping. Duke was too terrified to touch me at home, which I can't really blame him for, since his older brother reportedly has an ass full of buckshot from the first—and last—time he got into Kate Fullerton's pants.

I can't imagine how Dad would've reacted if he'd caught me and Duke going at it, but I can say it wouldn't have been pretty, or kind. So we went to his place most of the time instead. There was a higher chance of a kid wandering in on us, sure, but he also had a basement and a mom that slapped his ass and told him to wear a condom every time we went down there.

We didn't have to worry about being quiet, because upstairs was nothing short of a zoo. Duke had five younger siblings, and every one of them had an opinion about what the others should or should not be doing at any given time. There was constant shouting, chasing, and fighting over toys, occasionally overshadowed by the youngest screaming that she needed her diaper changed.

She always yelled "Shit" real loud, no matter what was actually in it.

But I heard lots of good things too, like one brother offering to fix his sister's doll when her head popped off, or the older girl changing the little one's pants because their mom had gone out in the yard to talk on the phone. Noise wasn't always a bad thing there, just a constant.

So when it stopped we always knew his dad had come home.

He wasn't a big guy, so we never heard his footsteps. It was the silence that spread out around him, like all the words floating around the kids had been sucked into him, leaving nothing behind.

Duke would tense beside me, and I'd hear the younger ones go to their rooms, doors closing behind them until dinnertime, which would be soon, because their mom didn't dare bring it to the table a minute late. It's like that now, here in the woods. I just scared the daylights out of every living thing, and it's the rage that they heard in me that's making them stay hid.

"Sorry," I say quietly, then lick my lips.

The truth is I got no business being out here. I'm way off-trail and in their territory, breaking brush and leaving blood and swear words behind me. I'm the scary thing in their house whose arrival brings quiet and hiding, hoping that they're not the one to catch its eye.

I don't want to ever be that to anybody or anything, so I nearly bite through my tongue to keep quiet as I get up. My foot's slipped out of the sling, so my leg straightens out, the knee going back to a place it hasn't been all day.

It hurts.

That hurts, and my foot hurts, and I know it's going to get worse before it gets better, but for now I've got one goal and that's water. I make it down to the stream, stumbling in and landing on all fours. It's so cold it takes my breath, the numbness working up past my wrists before I'm able to scramble onto a rock. I flex my fingers, forcing the blood to flow back through their deadened tips when I get smart and stick my foot in the water.

There's the shock of the pain first, water flowing *into* my foot and touching places that have never seen light. Dad always says if there's a way in, water will find it, something I'd usually hear when there was yet another leak in our roof, adding a new stain to our ceiling. I don't think he quite had the inside of his daughter's foot in mind when he said it, but damn, it's true.

Crushed nerves are drowned in the cold, screaming at the exposure then slowly deadening. I lean forward once it's fully numb, willing the same feeling into my thoughts as I peel back the bloodied sleeve to take a look.

My bones are a glossy white, like teeth poking through the gummy meat that surrounds them. I can't even call it a wound, really. It's a mashed mess of nerves and tendon and muscle. I've dressed enough deer in my life to know what's what in there, and I can't even begin to sort it out.

But under the moving water it's got a kind of beauty to it, something I can appreciate now that the pain is lessened. The water creates the illusion of movement, and I can almost imagine my toes are twitching, which means some things are still intact in there.

I pull my foot out of the current, the sun-warmed heat of the rock pleasant against the naked arch. Carefully, I slip the T-shirt bandage off my foot and pry around to see if I can get a sense of the damage. I press a little here, more firmly there, wondering if I'll be able to tell the difference if a bone is broken or not.

I'm down near the base of my two smallest toes when the slightest pressure from my fingers undoes all the good the cold did me. I can't even cry out, it hurts so bad, taking the wind right out of me just like Duke's dad does to his whole family. I make a weak gasp and clutch the side of the rock to keep from going on over into the drink and end up drowned like some drunk dipshit.

I stick my mangled bits back into the creek, let some of the pain subside before I look again. I don't fuck around, going right for the same spot that near killed me. I take a deep breath before I press down and am not surprised to see a stream of pus leak out from under what's left of the skin.

Something white coming out of you is only good if
you're a boy.

I've got an infection.

There's stuff I can eat out here; it's a question of if I've
got the nerve to do it.

Granted, I've had some things in my gut that maybe
shouldn't have been there: a pot roast gone a day too long,
the cockroach Meredith bet me five bucks I wouldn't eat
back in sixth grade. She did pay up. I can say a lot about
that girl, but she's honest.

I've never understood picky eaters, mostly because
I've always just been happy to have something to eat.
Growing up hungry has taught me a lot, and one of
those lessons was not to question what's put in front of
you. I remember one time Mom had something on the
table I couldn't quite put a name to. I came in from the
creek bed, mudded up to the knees, plopped down to a
plate of warm food, and said, "I'm not eating that."

Dad had set down his knife and fork real quiet and
said, "Then you're not hungry enough."

I get it now.

I get it because I just ate a worm.

It happened toward the evening, when I came across
another bit of running water. I had to wash my underwear and jeans because I'm still bleeding, so I thought

if I've got all that out to the breeze I might as well take my bra off too. Part of me thought maybe if I did, my shit-all luck would stay true to form and a group of hikers would show up. Or maybe a rescue chopper and a news crew.

Nobody came.

I stuck my foot in the water, mostly because I don't know what else to do about it, and leaned back against the bank, knocking loose a rock. It rolled down next to my hand, a big chunk of wet dirt stuck to the side, a marooned worm squirming like all get-out.

His world had shrunk so suddenly, I thought. A moment ago he could have gone anywhere, tunneling across this state and into the next. Now he's turning this way and that, wondering why there's nowhere to go and nothing but air to touch and a little bit of mud holding him in place. And then that was gone too, because I crumbled it away and popped him in my mouth before I could think too hard about it.

It moved in there, more curious than panicked, touching the side of my cheek. I grabbed a handful of water and threw everything back, like a child learning to swallow a pill for the first time. Then another. And another. Creek water flowed down my chin until I felt my stomach opening up, taking in what I'd just offered, way worse than anything Mom ever put in front of me.

It hurts.

I haven't had anything solid in my gut in two days. Every time I found water I drank until I could hear it sloshing in my belly, so I'm not exactly empty. But this is different. This is my body waking back up again, realizing it has a job, and that something needs to be digested.

It's like starting a car that's been dead for a while, the engine not turning over, everything grinding and putting up a fight because doing nothing is so much easier than doing something. That's what my body does, everything squeezing up tight in protest, not against the worm I put in my gut but because there's anything in there at all.

A little noise gets out of me, a sigh of acquiescence . . . and I think I'm in working order. I lean back again, a sheen of sweat cooling across my brow.

And then, dear God, I belch.

I'm trying not to think about Davey Beet.

That's hard because the only reason I'm not getting rained on right now is that he taught me how to make a shelter with nothing more than what nature could give me.

I was ten the year Dad sent me to camp and I'm old enough now to realize that the woman he'd been bringing around to watch baseball and have a beer with was more than just a friend, and he'd discovered what I'd learn years later—that there's no such thing as privacy in a trailer.

I didn't want to go. I stomped my feet and called him an asshole and told him he was abandoning me same as Momma did. Dad just pulled my hat down over my eyes and told me not to kick the boys in the balls and drove off, leaving me holding his old army rucksack and a pile of hurt feelings.

Throwing a fit didn't do a thing, and I was never the type for pouting. So I settled in at Camp Little Fish, a place where they taught me who Jesus was and I found someone I admired a hell of a lot more—Davey Beet.

Davey was a counselor and though he seemed ages older than the rest of the cabin leaders, I found out he was only fifteen and did the math on my fingers to figure out how old he would be when I could legally get married. And while I harbored that crush for the rest of my life, it deepened into something else on the first day he led a group of us into the forest—respect.

Davey carried a machete in his belt, using it to whack through brush and slice open a wild grapevine as thick as my arm. All us kids took a drink from the juice dripping out the end—not quite like something from the store but somehow better—and then he asked us if we wanted to learn how to stay dry in the rain, warm in the cold, and fed in the middle of nowhere.

He had my attention, which was a hard thing to get. I didn't like many people and found less worth talking to. But when Davey spoke I listened, and that's why I'm not getting soaked right down to my spine again tonight.

I heard thunder today in the midafternoon, low and rolling, far in the distance. The trees weren't kicking up a fuss yet, so I knew I had a little time. I found a big maple with a split down the middle, a place where twenty or thirty years ago two branches went their separate ways, creating a fork that I can prop a dead limb against. It's just above my head, and I need both hands to get it raised high enough, so I have to drop the walking stick and balance, my bad foot jammed in the sling and snug up against my ass.

It's not easy, and I'm shaky when I'm done, limp and pooling onto the ground. I land right where I unearthed the piece I lifted, uncovering grubs, fat and glistening. I would never say that they looked good to me, or that I didn't gag once or twice dry-swallowing them, but protein is protein, and if I'm going to finish building this thing I need something to digest other than my own stomach lining.

My gut clenches again, angry at being asked to do something once I've let it slumber. But I'm ready this time, and I let it have its way for a minute, kicking and screaming same as I did when Dad dragged me out of the truck and left me at Camp Little Fish.

I haul myself hand over hand and pick up my crutch. It started rubbing a sore spot this morning, a little nub from the curve that reaches around to the soft meat behind my armpit, digging in. It's like wearing the same bra too many days in a row and having the clasp leave a welt where it's gotten cozy against your skin. I knocked off that little knob against a tree and kept going, but all it did was start a new sore just below where the first one started.

I straighten for a second, letting all the muscles that have been hunched most of the day take a breath while I lean against the maple, eyeing everything around me for what I can use for the sides of my shelter.

Davey taught us how to do this, prop up the big center pole and then lean smaller branches against the side, tight against each other. The thunder rolls again, closer this time, and I hunch back over my walking stick, scuttling from one piece to the next and tossing them in the general direction of my shelter.

I get one side done and the other half up before the first sprinkle hits my nose, so part of the west wall is a shit job, and I don't think Davey would have much nice to say about it, but I got to get a covering over what I did manage to construct before the rain gets serious about what it's doing.

There's a dead pine a ways off, but that looks like a new development. An ash that the borers laid claim to fell across it lengthways, shearing off boughs slick as a razor blade. It's the best thing that's happened to me since my underwear dried all the way through. The needles aren't dead enough to fall away yet, so I drag limbs back to the shelter I'm making. They lie across the sticks I propped, like a grass roof that I layer some dead leaves on top of, and not a second too soon.

The next bit of thunder is more of a snap than a roll, a loud, brittle noise that I feel in my teeth. I grab the last thing I'm going to need, a flat piece of the ash that fell—wide as my hand and about half the length of my arm—and a broken branch off the same tree. I tuck them into my armpit and get back just as the rain starts, sliding under the lean-to I've made.

There's one thing I forgot to add on the list of things I've got: pants, shirt, underwear, bra—and my own hair. I yank it out a few strands at a time, rolling them together in my palms until they're twisted so tight nothing's going to break them loose. Then I tear out some more, lengthening and thickening the cordage as I roll it until I've got something that can pass for rope.

I'm not Rapunzel, and nobody could climb this, but it's good enough for what I need. I take the bit of ash branch and tuck the cordage into a split end, pressing the other against the flat piece. Then I start to spin it.

Davey Beet taught me to do this, years ago when he asked if anyone knew how to make a fire. I watched him spin a branch against a flat piece of wood, fingers pulling down on a bit of string he nocked through the top, pushing down and spinning at the same time, the sinewy muscles of his arms distracting me for a full minute. This may be where my fascination with boys' arms started, come to think of it.

Physics applies no matter where you are in the world, and Davey Beet made fire in the woods with nothing but friction, his face red and arms shaky with effort by the time a bit of smoke rose up, but he did it. Then he showed us how.

I was the only one that managed to follow his example that day, and I've done it since because it's not a skill you want to lose. I'd never tried it with nothing but grubs and a worm in my stomach and half a foot open to the world, but science is a solid thing, and I get a thin line of smoke just in time, right before my arms are about to give out. I feed it with dead leaves and a puff of my breath, my heart thrilling at the sight of a spark, then the lick of a flame. I'm not going to starve, and I'm not going to be cold, and it's all because of Davey Beet.

And the reason why I don't want to think about that is because he's more than likely dead.

* * *

Davey Beet walked into the Smokies with a full pack and a broken heart, his girl having gone off to college and found something that fit her better than already broken-in shoes. I was twelve and ready to show off what I had, packing only tank tops and ripped jean shorts in my bag for Camp Little Fish, a few years before he left.

But it was my brain Davey liked. He was seventeen by then, running a whole program about trail survival. I signed up for it the day I got to camp, hoping he'd notice me as I stood there uncapping a Sharpie and putting my name big and bold, first one on the poster for his class.

He saw me, sure, but it wasn't my boobs that he cared about. Davey was a good guy, and while there were plenty of others who might take a look at something too young to touch (and some that didn't mind taking the risk of touching something that was illegal), all he cared about was my mind.

And my attitude.

Davey started calling me Ass-kicker Ashley the second year I went back to Little Fish, when I bashed a fellow camper on the back of a head with a stick for putting a toad in the fire. He said he just did it to see what would happen, so I used the same line of defense, although I could hardly claim surprise at the trickle of blood that had seeped from behind his ear after my first swing. I also can't blame pure curiosity once the discovery had been made and I took a second swing anyway.

The directors would've sent me home, but no one could get ahold of Dad, and I didn't know Momma's phone number, so they had to keep me. I was separated from the other kids, which was fine because they were all a bunch of assholes anyway. That's when Davey took to calling me Ass-kicker Ashley and showed me how to set a snare.

So when he saw me come back that third year, all leggy and sunburned and taking my time writing out my name in cursive on his class roster, he smiled and asked if I wanted to know what plants I could eat and which ones would kill me in return. I fought down the blush rising in my already burned skin and told him hell yes. He took the Sharpie from me and scribbled out my last name, writing *Ass-kicker* in front of my first.

"That way I know who it is," he said.

I was the only one who signed up for that class. Everyone else wanted to take ceramics and something about jewelry. They sent an adult out there with us—whether for the sake of propriety or because the directors were afraid I might have a habit of hitting people with sticks, I don't know. But our escort usually fell asleep under a tree, sitting so still that at one point we came back from a hike to find a snake sunning in his lap.

For a week I had Davey Beet to myself, and while I know I didn't do a good job hiding my childish crush, he never acknowledged it, keeping up a steady stream of bird identification, toxic toads, and what mushrooms I'd better never, ever touch unless I wanted them growing out of my spine a week later, a not-too-good smell coming out of my corpse.

He taught me how to track too, then made me turn my back while he walked away, with instructions to yell three times if I got freaked out and thought I was lost. He said he'd come for me if that happened, and there were a few times while I tracked him that I wanted to call out, but pride kept it down. That, and I'd spot the next sign, a step or two ahead. A bent twig, a turned leaf, a muddy slip where he didn't get traction.

I found him twice, the third time he went down to the creek and circled behind me, pushing me in when I heard his footstep a second too late. I'd shrieked and splashed him, tickled pink that he'd touched me, even if it was just in fun. We waited for the water to settle and then laid on our bellies on the bank, Davey plucking a fish out with his bare hands, easy as pie. (Momma always hated that saying. She said pie is actually pretty hard, especially the crust part.)

Davey knew everything and could do it all, so when I heard his girl split I was half-elated, and half-pissed-off because I knew how it hurt to be left. I wanted to tell him so, but there was no way to do it. I didn't have his number, because the camp was real strict about interaction between campers and counselors, and he lived two towns over. The local paper ran a story about him doing a leg of the AT on his own, with a big picture of him smiling in a way that didn't look quite right, no teeth, dimples not popping.

I said I was going to cover two miles today. I bet I didn't even put in one.

Davey Beet taught me everything I know about survival, and he never came back out of these woods.

So what chance do I have?

DAY THREE

A possum is never cute. They're one of the rare animals that even has ugly-ass babies. Dad told me once that possums are loners because they're smart enough not to live in the same area as another possum so they're not competing for food, but I think it's 'cause they can't stand looking at each other. Regardless, that face doesn't look good on anything, and it's even worse when it's the first thing I see when I wake up.

It doesn't help that it's chewing on my foot.

"MOTHERFUCKER!" I yell, grabbing for the first thing my hand comes to, which happens to be a stick. The possum is long gone by the time I pitch it, clocking my foot instead and sending a wave of pain through my body that leaves me sweating in the pale light of early morning.

Shit.

There's a lot of problems with what just happened. For one thing, a possum bit me. Getting chewed by anything is never good, no matter what did it or where they got you. What bothers me way more is that I didn't feel it.

I crawl out from my shelter, knees dragging through the ashes of the fire I made the night before. The sun is barely there; mist not yet burned off hangs all around me. Walking is like swimming, my face wet and hair stuck to my neck by the time I get down to the stream.

Something bolts as I slide down the bank, something big enough that brush moves in its wake, and birds break from their slumber. But I don't see any prints other than deer and raccoon in the soft mud, so I find a good spot to learn bad news.

I set my crutch aside and strip the T-shirt bandage from my foot. The smell gets me first. I'd noticed it yesterday, but it was hard to pinpoint, and in spring all kinds of things are rotting in the woods. Everything that died during the winter waits a few months to rot, and then those of us that made it through get to smell the result. Spring is funny that way, popping with life and color as bulbs come up and trees flower. But underneath it all is a scummy film of death, if you know how to spot it.

I know.

I think maybe deep down I knew it yesterday but didn't want to think too hard on it. Once, when I went grocery shopping with our first-of-the-month check I grabbed a can of tuna that should've never made the shelf. I was pushing my cart, trying to find a way around the old lady on a scooter in front of me because, damn, she was rank.

I drove home with a wrinkled nose and bad words in my mouth because apparently just moving through her stink had been enough for me to carry a whiff around with me. It wasn't until I was carrying a bag into the trailer that I realized it was my punctured tuna can that smelled the whole time, and that old lady had probably been pushing that electric motor to its limits to try to get away from *me*.

And now here I am in the woods, thinking something had to go and die where I camped for the night and the whole time it's my own foot rotting at the end of my leg.

"Dammit," I say, looking down at what's left of me.

There are teeth marks in my fourth toe, and my pinkie is almost gone.

"This little piggy cried, 'wee, wee, wee,'" I say to myself, grimly touching the stump of what used to be my toe.

Possums are industrous scavengers, but they're also too lazy to kill things themselves. They'd rather snack on someone else's kill two days after they were done with it than do the job themselves. That's what the possum thought I was—dead meat, carrion, remains.

And I guess it was half-right.

The crushed part of my foot is a sick shade of gray, something I didn't notice by firelight. The skin is cold and doesn't move when I touch it, refusing to make soft ridges and rolls the way Duke's back always did when I gave him a rub.

My foot is a dead thing. Not bleeding. Unfeeling.

I bend down and sniff, coming back up real quick when I get a nose full of the stink I'm giving off. Between this and still bleeding like a stuck pig I'm going to attract all kinds of things wanting to take a bite.

I pull up my pant leg to see that predators are the least of my worries.

There's a strain of red running up to my ankle, the swell of hot infection close behind. I stick my foot in the stream and lean back to look at the sky.

It's going to have to come off.

Like the worm whose world went from unlimited to a small piece of dirt to the inside of my stomach, my world has changed drastically. The first day out all I thought of was home. I would break out of the trees onto the road, hobble along until a driver found me, hitch a ride into town, get my foot seen to, then go to my own bed and lie down in it. The second day I was hoping to hit the trail, looking for white blazes. Now I'm picking a tree, taking a rest when I get to it, then aiming for another one.

Yesterday I wanted to make two miles. Today I'm just aiming for the next maple.

All I can do is hope I'm headed somewhat west. The clouds have been constant, a thick gray haze that won't let me get a good read on the sun, make much use of a shadow stick, or allow its rays to ever really warm me. When I do get sweaty it's a slick kind of feeling, like maybe I'm sweating not because I'm too hot but because I'm getting sick.

My foot is back in the sling, up off the ground. Even though I know it doesn't matter one way or the other to the dead part, the living tissue is swelling, and keeping it elevated is the only thing I can really do right now. When I set out this morning, the crutch rubbing the raw spot on my back, I was thinking I had to get somewhere—now.

Like maybe I'd been playing the last two days, having an adventure. Like maybe I could just decide to find the trail, then the road, then help. None of that's true, and so by midday I'm in a puddle under an oak, my chest hitching as I decide whether I'm going to cry.

I landed near a pile of clovers, which is lucky not because any of them have four leaves but because they're edible. I pull it up by the handful, chewing and swallowing carefully while my stomach complains again.

Clover can keep me from starving, but I'm burning off more than I'm taking in, covering miles with a rotten foot and not much in my stomach. I won't die from hunger, but I'm not going to put on any weight either. I noticed this morning that my pants were sagging more than usual, hugging hips that aren't quite what they used to be. My body has already started digesting itself, breaking down my fat reserves and using them to keep me moving.

Next it'll move on to muscles.

And I need those.

"Shit," I say to the sky, watching a break in the cloud cover overhead. I've got to get back up, move forward even though I don't know what I'm moving toward. The only thing I can say for sure is that I haven't seen a hint of another human being for days. Never in my life have I wished for litter, but a forgotten water bottle or tossed pop can wouldn't be taken amiss right now. Usually that stuff is all over. Cans. Bottles. Chip bags and candy wrappers. Anything people can carry and eat and leave behind, they do.

Duke and I hated it, this casual disrespect. Anybody that loved the woods enough to come spend time in it ought to know better than to trash it. But there was always something blowing in the wind or floating past in the stream, stuff that won't break down in a million years, only get bleached out by the sun, its color the one thing to leave naturally.

That's why I used to wander sometimes, if Duke wasn't with me. I'd start somewhere on public land, but there's not always an easy way to tell when you've stepped into private areas—and to be honest I was never looking too hard for signs anyway. Places with no people—or the leavings of them—were sacred to me, offering a distinct sense of being alone that I couldn't achieve with power walkers moving past me, neon shoes flashing as they bitched about their neighbors.

I guess I was always looking for solitude.

I've got that now, in spades.

"You've got to get up," I say aloud, hoping it'll be more motivating that way.

It's true, whether I only say it in my head or put a voice to it. There's no energy left in me, no strength in my legs or my arms, but I do it anyway because I've decided that's what I'm going to do, and I can be stubborn.

Living things will fight to stay that way.

When I was little we had a trampoline, a ratty old one that some relative thought trashed up their yard so they *donated* it to us out of the kindness of their pinched, tiny hearts. I loved it, and Dad could give less of a shit about the yard, so I spent most of the summer I turned eleven trying to see if I could bounce myself onto the roof of the trailer. I managed once, and Dad came out red in the face, told me I was likely to fall right through the ceiling and then how much rain would come in?

After that, I kept to aiming for branches of the elm that hung nearby, grabbing one when I could reach it and hanging there for as long as my bony little arms could take it. I was right at the quivering stage and about to let go when I spotted a raccoon moving through the field across the way.

It was moving slow and funny, and it was bright daylight. You don't see a raccoon during the day unless there's something wrong with it, and this one had more than a few problems.

Distemper was the first.

The second was a buzzard following behind, waiting for him to die.

He walked, patient as anything, matching the sick coon step for step. The raccoon knew it was there, kept looking over his shoulder every now and then. I dropped from the elm, ran inside, and grabbed Daddy's twelve-gauge. There wasn't anything left of that buzzard but a beak and a few feathers after I took my shot.

Then I put the raccoon out of his misery.

I wanted him to see that buzzard die first. Wanted him to know that every step he'd taken with death on his heels hadn't been taken in vain. He'd fought for each one, walking toward nothing but knowing that he couldn't stop. So I let him see it was worth it, in the end.

Now here I am, doing the same.

And I admit, I have taken to looking over my shoulder to make sure nothing is following me.

I come across water about a mile later, and a nice rocky overhang that I can sleep under tonight in case it rains again. It's not late yet, barely evening, but I've got nothing left in me except tears, so I collapse next to the water, not so much drinking as opening up my mouth and letting water flow into it.

There's a bit of purslane clinging to the rocky bank, and some tendrils of wild grapevine hang down from the maple they've climbed. It's too early for them to have fruit, but the leaves are edible, as is the purslane. The rule with plants is everything tastes better boiled, but while I have water and I can make fire, I don't have any-thing to boil in.

I make another fire, burning a hole next to the first one in my fireboard, hoping I don't have to make too many more before all this is said and done. I can't even raise my arms by the time I get a flame, so I just sit, using my good foot to scoot dead leaves toward the lit-tle fire I've got going while I wait for some strength to return. Enough to gather some wood. Enough to keep me from shivering tonight, which is nothing but a waste of energy.

I lie down before full dark, curled around the little bit of fire I managed to make, my head in my arms. I've scooted out past the edge of the overhang so I can see the stars, and there among them, a red, blinking dot.

It's a plane, three miles above me and moving fast, everyone on board fed and warm, healthy and safe. They're thinking about where they're going or where they've come from, the people they've left or are going to. It's the closest I've been to another human being in days, and they have no idea I'm down here.

Dying.

DAY FOUR

In the morning my foot is so bad I can smell it without bringing it to my nose, which means anything else can too. I didn't wake to anything chewing on me, but there was a rustling in the brush when I slid out from under the overhang in the morning to take a piss. I try to be careful, but I'm weak as a kitten and manage to pee on myself a little. I'd rather smell like urine than death though. One will keep the critters away. The other will bring them in for a meal.

I strip off my clothes and slip into the creek. I smell like old blood and dried sweat, layered on top of death and piss. I wash as best I can, checking the line of mud I drew on my leg last night. The red streaks have marched past it as I slept, the spread of infection reaching up my calf. The swelling follows, leaving skin swollen and tight.

This is how I measure time, with no clock and the sun perpetually hidden. There is no such thing as minutes or hours, only the freckle on my leg, the scar beneath it, and how long it will take for the red fingers of inflammation to reach them.

The answer is *not long*.

And the follow-up is *even less* if I get a fever that weakens me.

Yesterday I was thinking that if I'd been treating this whole thing like a test of my abilities, I needed to pass it real soon. After looking at my foot, I put the deadline a little closer, edging up on me just like the red on my leg.

Urgency leads me to head off in clothes still wet from the creek, adding to the weight I bear and chafing against my legs. I cannot wait for them to dry. Cannot wait for the sun and wind to do me favors. Cannot stop to try to catch a fish, because infinite patience is required to snatch one from the water with only your hands, and I have neither infinity nor patience.

What I have is a bomb on the end of my leg. Not one that will explode but rather expand, licking its poison into my healthy tissue until I am no longer well enough to walk. And once that happens, I'm done.

I've given myself until the swelling hits the scar on

my calf, the remnant of a deep cut from the steel siding
of a neighbor's trailer that opened me down to the muscle when I was trick-or-treating, my Wonder Woman
cape getting stuck in between the stacked cinder blocks
they used for steps.

I pulled my sock up and told them I was fine, because
they were a nice old couple that gave out whole candy
bars instead of bite-size, and I'd never had a whole
candy bar to myself in my life. I limped home, shoe full
of blood, and ate the candy bar in the back of the truck
while Dad took me to the urgent care where they charge
only half what the ER does and do stitches as good as
anybody else.

I'm searching the sky for a break in the trees.

I'm listening for the sound of a car.

And God help me, I'm looking for flint.

Because I can't take my foot off without it.

Trees are thieves.

They take things from you quietly, swiping a bandanna from your ponytail or a hair tie from your wrist.
I've seen hundred-dollar sunglasses hanging off maples,
and water bottles snagged on low-hanging willows, their
wispy fingers pulling things from hikers' packs without
them knowing they lost something until they need it.

I spot the hat while I'm looking for a break in the

canopy, hoping to see an open area that means there's a road ahead. The hat is just out of my reach, which means the tree stole it years ago, and it's been hanging there waiting for its owner to come back. Meanwhile it travels higher, the tree claiming it forever.

But not from me.

I want that hat, so I'm going to get it.

I whack at the branch it's stuck on with my walking stick, taking a few inexpert swings. I miss the first time and land on my front the next, grinding my own curled fist into my stomach and sending the dandelions I ate earlier back up into my throat. I swallow fast because I'm not in a position to be wasting anything. Then I get back up and try again.

It's the fifth swing, my ninth swear, and a good gust of wind that does it. The hat lands at my feet, and I follow it down to the ground, happy to finally win at something, and happier yet to rest. I'm sweating and exhausted, cursing myself for a fool to have wasted so much strength on something stupid.

But I wanted that hat, and I got it.

And I wanted it because it's Davey Beet's.

No one ever found him.

They sent in search parties and sniffer dogs, family and friends, ex-girlfriends and enemies trying to make better what had gone wrong. I wanted to go, but Dad wouldn't let me, too aware of my confidence and my connection to the missing. Dad was afraid I'd go into the woods after Davey Beet, his girl hero come to save the day but gets lost in the woods and ends her own life. Davey was so gone it was like he never was, even if I could still look at his picture in the camp mailing I kept every spring when it showed up in the mailbox.

Rumors started, some people saying he went in there with no intention of ever coming out, others saying that no way the woods got the better of Davey Beet, that he'd come home any day now with a great story and a better smile.

I was a fervent believer in the latter.

I blew up at Stephanie's cousin over the campfire for saying a bear got Davey, because while that was something that could have happened, it's an option that leaves no room for doubt. In my mind, Davey Beet is alive and well, using all he's got to walk these woods and make a way for himself, maybe trying to find his way home, maybe not. To me, whatever Davey decided to do was the right call, and I bet the bears ran away from *him*.

It got to be an issue between me and Duke, the way I held Davey up in my mind. One time when we were hiking we hit a spur neither one of us knew too well. There was a lonely trail sign stuck into the ground, showing the length of it but not clarifying the distance. I took one glance and told him no way we could do that spur and get back before dark, and neither one of us had flashlights.

Duke said it was fine; the spur didn't seem that long to him. Three hours later we were hustling it, flashing our phones on when we needed them to spot the blazes, trying to conserve batteries. We broke out onto the trailhead past midnight, thirsty, exhausted, covered in bug bites, leg muscles flickering from the pace. We'd had to pick it up after dark fell, and more than once we heard things larger than us moving off-trail. I'd kept my mouth shut the whole time, knowing that arguing about whose fault it was wasn't going to get us home any faster.

But my silence irritated Duke just as much as if I'd said anything, and when we climbed into his old truck, I didn't get an apology for what could have been a tense night in the woods. Instead I got his jealousy, all stopped up and simmering from every word I'd ever said about Davey that he let pass by.

"I know what you're thinking," Duke had said, knuckles white on the steering wheel as he drove me home. "You're thinking if you were hiking with Davey Beet he would've known better than to take that spur."

My own anger jumped up at that, for one thing

because I hadn't said a goddamn sideways word to Duke even though he could've gotten us killed, and another because I didn't like the way he said Davey Beet's name, like it tasted bad.

So I hit back, hard.

"If I'd been hiking with Davey Beet, I wouldn't've minded spending the night in the woods."

It was a low blow, and it hit him right where it was meant to. Duke didn't talk to me for a few days, but we picked up like it had never happened when he came to my door with fishing poles and a can of worms. For my part, I did try not to mention Davey quite as much, even when Duke was casting wrong and I knew Davey could've done it better.

But Davey Beet was never far from my mind, now or in the time when he first went missing.

I sat in Dad's recliner (the foot permanently flipped up because it got stuck that way) watching the news every night for a week. Davey was the lead story, then a follow-up, then a late mention. Soon he was dropped entirely, because there was nothing to say anymore. Hope had faded, just like the pattern in the knit cap I'm holding now.

He kept it clipped to the side of his pack even in the summer, because he said he never knew if he was going to stay out all night, and it could get chilly in the woods after dark no matter what the season was. His mom had made it for him, carefully counting stitches as she wove tan yarn into brown, knitting antlers into her son's hat. Davey told me it was the nicest thing anyone had ever done for him, even if she did only think of her son as an eight-point.

I put it on my head now, though I'm sweating.

I'm wearing the only thing anyone has seen of Davey Beet in two years.

People have been using flint since forever to start fires and make tools, to kill animals and each other. I'm not aiming to kill anything—including myself—and while having some tools would be nice, I'm not exactly fixing to stay around long enough to build a house. What I need is a good edge on something with enough weight behind it to go clear through my foot.

I'm half hoping to find it, half hoping not to.

It's taken the better part of the day, and I've sweated right through Davey Beet's hat, but I'm not taking it off because I know another tree will steal it. I follow the sound of running water when I notice the shadows getting longer, take a few deep drinks and check my leg again. My scar is a white blaze surrounded by red, the skin around it puffed and itching.

"Shit," I say, and stick my whole leg into the water to cool it off while I think.

Mostly, I'm thinking about running.

It's a dumb thing to worry about when I can't even walk, but running became an obsession after that first practice, when I had to show Coach that I could do it, and then the next, when I had to show him I could do better. It's a sport that we could afford—no equipment needed except a good pair of shoes. Even that could sometimes push Dad's worry lines a little deeper, but after I broke the state record in cross-country Coach started buying shoes for me out of the athletic fund.

And thank God, because I'd go through two or three pairs in a season, running to practice, running at practice, and then running home. I ran on the weekends, got up early and ran in the mornings. I'd run to school and half the time beat the bus there. The wind in my ears meant I couldn't hear nothing else, and that was just fine.

But there were things I did kind of like hearing; my name on the announcements at school when I placed at a big invitational, everybody's reaction at my face in the paper when I made it to nationals as a sophomore. Davey Beet even wrote me a letter about that, the handwriting careful and neat, as were the words. I wrote him back right away, but it was a community college mail-box and he had dropped out before my letter reached him. It came back to me, "Return to Sender" stamped in red ink.

Getting a letter from Davey Beet was the high point in my life until a man in a windbreaker walked up to me after a meet and asked if I was considering going to college and where. I eyed him funny for a second, until my coach cut in and I realized I was talking to a scout.

The idea that there was a college out there that might have a spot in it for me had never even been the whiff of a dream. I went home with paperwork and talked to Dad, and we both cried a bit, and when I signed at the end of junior year the local *and* county papers showed up to take pictures. The truth is that there's a full-ride scholarship in my feet, and one of them coming off doesn't mean I get half the money.

It means I get none.

"Shit," I say again, and pull my leg from the water.

I'm nearly numb, so it doesn't hurt as bad when I press against the skin, leaving white indentations behind. The crushed part of my foot is gray and dead, but I'll have to cut where the tissue is still alive if I've got any hope of stopping this infection.

It'll hurt. But that's not what worries me. What worries me is that I'll cut off part of my body and wake up tomorrow to find out I was half a mile from somebody's house, and that I threw away college and any chance of being anything other than a washed-up athlete in a small town because I didn't know it.

All the time I've been out here I've been thinking in longer terms, bigger goals. When I find the road . . . when I get to the hospital . . . when they fix my foot . . . this will all be like it never happened. But I don't think I'm anywhere near a road, or a hospital. The only thing of those three here right now is my foot, and it's going to kill me. It's the right now I got to be thinking about, real hard.

I pull Davey Beet's hat down over my face, to shut out the world for a while.

"I don't know what to do," I admit.

It gets hot under there fast, so I pull it back up, and the first thing I see is a nice hefty piece of flint sticking out of the bank opposite me.

"Well, fuck you too," I say.

Momma told me once that I was born with teeth.

It's one of the few things I remember real clear about her, mostly because she made it sound like I chewed my way out of her rather than being born the normal way. For the longest time I watched barn cats giving birth, wondering why they didn't seem to mind so much. I learned later that humans are the only mammals that experience terrible pain when giving birth, something they told me at Camp Little Fish was Eve's fault, but I thought it sounded more like poor planning on God's part. When I said so Davey Beet laughed until his face was red as his last name, and I was blushing too because he'd noticed me.

Dad told Momma she didn't need to be telling me that story anymore, and there was a big fight—one of the last ones. She told him he didn't have no idea what it was like to carry a child for the better part of a year, almost die getting it out, and then have it not need her anymore. He told her to shut her mouth and stop making me feel bad for doing nothing worse than being born, and that if I was born with teeth it was because I came out ready to defend myself, and there wasn't any shame in that.

So I was kind of proud of it, actually. When I told Meredith, she called me a liar, so I knocked her down on the playground and her mom called mine. I listened in on the conversation, Momma using an old wall phone with a cord she'd wrap around and around her arm while she talked. She started out apologizing for me—something she'd gotten good at, I guess—but then after a few drinks of Wild Turkey she was telling Meredith's mom all about the teeth, and how I was born with fingernails long as Tammy Faye Bakker's.

Momma said she could feel me inside her, running my nails across her ribs, exploring the inside of her body the same as I do the woods now. She said she knew I was a wild thing and was surprised when I started walking early because it would've been more fitting for me to stay on all fours my whole life. I busted in then and told her I walked early so I could run sooner, all to get away from her and her endless bitching.

I got a smack across the mouth for that, but I guess I kind of deserved it.

I'm using those nails now to dig out this chunk of flint from the creek bank, and damn if it isn't perfect for what I need it to do. It's got an edge already, one I can sharpen by knapping off a slice with another rock. Once again, the world is telling me to cut into my own flesh because instead of exploding into a bunch of tiny pieces when I hit it, the flint breaks clean, making an edge sharp enough to slice my finger pad. The whole thing fits in my hand nicely, the edge of a tooth that isn't mine, but only hungers for what I've got. When I hold it I become a weapon, my arm an ax handle, the flint a good blade. I can hack off the bad part of my foot with this; I know it.

Still, I delay.

I walk clear into early evening, ignoring a rainstorm

that kicks up and soaks me, pushing forward and hoping for a house, a road, someone's wandering dog that I can follow home. But there is nothing and no one, and soon I realize I'm singing a song from my childhood, one that I always loved.

The bear went over the mountain
The bear went over the mountain
The bear went over the mountain . . .
And what do you think he saw?

That poor fucker saw another mountain, and while I'm not climbing peaks exactly they may as well be for all the effort it's taking. My foot is hot and heavy in the sling, my knee screaming about being bent for so long, my arms shaky and a fresh trickle of blood running down my side from where the crutch has flat punctured my back. I got nothing to look forward to but self-dismemberment and maybe seeing another mountain, and I'm so much more into my singing than thinking about that I don't realize I'm going over the edge of a ridge until too late.

I roll, ass over teakettle, my hand clenching tight onto my chunk of flint and the other gripping my crutch because these are the most valuable things I own. My foot slips free of the sling, my leg bending hard under me as I crash into the little trickle of water at the bottom. I am nothing but nerves, hot and severed, a warm bag of skin filled with pain. I can't even make a noise, I hurt so bad, like the inhale of a baby right before it throws a rip-roaring fit, a moment of silence to consider what's about to come.

There aren't even swears for how I feel right now, or enough languages to cover it. I stare up at the sky and let pain have its way, rain starting to spatter my face. I'm considering just lying here until the water rises enough to cover my mouth, then my nose. Then the clouds part for a moment, and a ray of light breaks through, pointing like a spotlight. At camp they called those Jesus clouds, but they're not landing on Christ right now; the heavens opened for me so that I could find a meth lab.

Meth smells like ass.

I know this because my uncle Chuck went into what he called a "business venture" a few years ago, and my dad called a "federal offense." Dad didn't like it too much when Chuck handed me and Duke each a wad of bills and asked us to keep an eye on a trailer he set up out in the woods. He said since we were minors we couldn't get slapped with anything too serious and he'd been sure to put the lab out on public land so that we could claim we were just wandering if anybody official ever showed up.

Dad was not happy with my new job, but Chuck said he owed him one. Apparently back in the nineties Uncle Chuck told my dad wouldn't it be great to start a business where you rented your DVDs to people, mailed the DVDs to them, and they mailed them back and it'd be better than running to the video store and easy money besides. He had it all worked out until Dad told him it was stupid, and nobody wanted to rent somebody else's porn anyway, and then Netflix happened and Uncle Chuck hasn't really forgiven him.

So that's how I got a job guarding a meth lab, but I didn't dare touch the stuff or I knew Dad would kill me. Given the messes I saw coming to buy, I wasn't in a big hurry to try it. Chuck paid us pretty good, and Duke and I would just sit out there in our lawn chairs, him smoking weed while we talked. I earned enough to buy myself a real nice backpack, but then a bigger dealer than Uncle Chuck got word of his little lab and we found it torched one day, Chuck lying off in the brush with the shit kicked out of him.

The setup I've discovered looks to be about the same type of deal as Uncle Chuck's, but smaller. It's a little pop-up camper, pulled in here so long ago that the tracks are gone and any brush that got whacked down in the process has sprung back up and done a few years of growing in the meantime. It's even up on blocks, which tells me whoever is running things has been doing so for a while and feels secure enough to stay.

Which means I'm in the ass middle of nowhere.

The door's locked, but I kick it in with my good leg just as the storm gets a second wind, letting down a sheet of rain that makes the roof on this thing sing louder than I did after my foot got crushed. I drag myself into the camper, pushing the door shut behind me just in time. A wall of water hits the side of the camper so hard I feel it shift on the blocks and cross my fingers that I'm not about to go back over the ridge and die, crushed in a meth lab. It settles back into place and so does my stomach, so I take a minute to catch my breath.

I know enough about the cooking process to know this place hasn't been used in a while. All the cook stuff—beakers, flasks, pans—is pushed off to the side of the counter, and scummy from the last use that never got washed away. I get to my feet and start opening cupboards, hoping somebody used this place enough to have some food squirreled away.

That's when I find the pills.

Apparently, they decided to upgrade.

The cupboards are lined with orange prescription

bottles, the labels torn away. Some are full, some only have a few pills, but there's enough here to get the whole county high as a kite, and their dogs too. There's also an old Whitman's candy tin full of cash, the bills filthy and lumped together, making it clear that it's a dirty business but it's a good one too, because there's enough here to probably send me to college even if I lost both my legs right up to the hip.

I put it back, wiping my hands on my jeans.

More useful to me is a box of granola bars, six months expired and likely to break my teeth, but it's food, and deeply needed. I crawl onto the bare mattress and find a moldy blanket shoved down between it and the wall. As night takes over day I curl into a ball and huddle under it, chewing on granola until my gums bleed.

My brain gives me a break, a much-needed reprieve from reality. It must know that I'm safe here because it's the first time I've slept deep enough to dream, and it must also know what I need, because I dream about running.

Laney Uncapher went to a school better than mine, had higher cheekbones than me and longer legs to go with them. Her cross-country team had extra trainers, expensive uniforms, and one of those tents that has rooms in it that they used when they traveled. I hated her on principle, and she hated me because I kept beating her.

It started in junior high, our county small enough that we knew the faces on the other teams by then, some of them friendly, some of them not. We found out quick that we were the front-runners, breaking out of the starting line and keeping our lead on the sorry sacks behind us the whole time. High school came, and we traded in two miles for 5Ks every weekend, and a few scattered into the week for good measure. Always we were neck and neck, me and Laney, hers cleaner than mine, I'll admit.

When she pops up in my dream I'm almost glad to see her just because it's another human face. She gives me the side-eye she always did as I paced her, both of us spitting when it would hit the other, even blowing out a snot rocket for good measure if we knew the wind was just right. I let her have the lead on a hill, because I know the burst of energy she uses on the climb will cost her later, and I've got enough in the tank to turn it on at the end. We take a curve, and I'm not at my old course anymore, the way a dream takes you, I'm back at the state qualifiers junior year and we're headed for the woods.

Those woods caused me some trouble, same as the one I'm in now is doing. The papers had been talking up this rivalry, setting us up as country mouse and city mouse, and doesn't everybody love an underdog (or mouse)? I was that exactly, and I'd been under for so much of my life in everything but running that I was taking this and no questions asked.

But Laney started in right at the line, all of us girls hopping in place, jogging, or leaning on each other's shoulders as we pulled our heels back to our asses. I had ahold of Kavita and was stretching out my quads when Laney got close enough to make sure I'd hear her.

"Pretty windy," she said to one of her teammates as they stretched, her blond fishtail braid lying alongside her in the grass.

"Lean into it," her friend said, pulling her toes back toward her shoulders to give her calf muscle a tweak.

"Not worried about me," Laney said, making sure to catch my eye. "I'm thinking it might be enough to blow all the trash away."

"Too bad it can't gust enough to pick up a whore," I said, and Kavita put her forehead on mine, pulling my gaze to her.

"You stop that, Ashley Hawkins," she said, dark eyes intent on mine. "You're better than her on the course. Be better than her off it."

It took me by surprise, as Kavita wasn't one to correct me; she usually left that to Meredith. But she expected more of me when I had my uniform on, I guess, and I know I let her down because Laney had me on that curve, and I was a few strides behind her going into the woods.

That course has always been a tough one, and the woods was a nice breather of flat ground, speckled in shade. Coaches didn't worry about their runners needing them on that leg, so they never followed us in, and the course was too skinny for spectators there. We were alone, me and Laney Uncapher, way ahead of everybody else, when she glanced over her shoulder and gave me a smile.

It was a bitch-ass smile, and a poor choice on her part, because it fired quicker than tinder in my gut and I shot off after her, not thinking about winning, or college, or anything other than hurting her, bad.

I came out of the woods first.

I heard steps behind me and recognized them as Kavita's. She caught up to me and, without a word, reached down her front and pulled out the handkerchief she always carried with her when she ran because she was too classy to blow it all over the course. I held it to my split lip and pressed until it stopped bleeding, wiped off the runnels of blood that had slipped down my neck and into my cleavage, and gave it back to Kavita. She fell back and I went ahead, glancing over my shoulder once to see her doing the same thing for Laney, whose left eye was swollen shut.

I won that race, but damn if I felt good about it.

Kavita never said a thing to me, which was worse than the reaming Coach gave me afterward. Laney got it too. They put us shoulder to shoulder and chewed us out until they had even less air than we did, but neither one of us opened our mouths. We settled it our own way, and we both knew it wasn't over yet.

Except it was, because she got pregnant and now I'm lost in the woods and the last time I saw Laney Uncapher she had one eye shut and the other staring me down begging my fist to close the other.

She doesn't look that way in my dream. Laney's healthy and strong, and farther ahead of me than she ever was in any race. She looks back over her shoulder as she heads into the shadows, but there's no smile this time, only worry, and when I get into the trees she's nowhere to be found. Laney's not in front of me, and Kavita isn't behind. I'm alone in the woods.

Even in my dreams.

DAY FIVE

The pill bottles aren't labeled, but I've been to enough parties to know what oxy looks like. I count out four and set them next to the bottle of whiskey I found under the mattress. I chew my way through another granola bar, so starved that I can feel the energy it gives me right away.

I find the biggest flask—an Erlenmeyer—a word I learned in sixth grade and liked so much I kept it in my head, and go down to the trickle of water I landed in the day before. It's higher now, with a pushing strength from yesterday's rains that threatens to take the flask from my hand if I don't hold on tight. I clean it out as best I can, shoving a leaf down inside and using a stick to scrub it around, little bits of scum floating free in the water as I work. It's as clean as it's going to get, and anything else I do would be procrastination, pure and simple.

I set up my operating room in the camper, taking off my shirt and soaking it in whiskey to clean part of the floor. Then I slug back a mouthful along with an oxy. From what I've seen at parties it'll take about half an hour for it to hit me, so I've just set a timetable for myself. I rest my foot on the cleaned bit of floor and tear another strip off my shirt.

I know there are blood vessels all through my foot, probably some arteries too, but I don't know where, or how long I should leave a tourniquet on in the first place. I stick my fingers—already shaky, I notice—along different spots of my foot and leg, hoping to find a place where my pulse is stronger. But I'm such a swollen mess everything feels lumpy, and I think I could find my heartbeat in my big toe if I pinched hard enough. In the end I pick a spot above my ankle and tie off my shirt tight, ignoring the rush of pain as it sinks into the puffed flesh.

I straighten up the line of necessities beside me on the floor: the oxy and whiskey, the flint, Erlenmeyer of water, two granola bars, and Davey Beet's hat. I position the only pillow I could find right where I'm assuming I'll fall over afterward and take a good, hard look at my foot.

Some more digging had turned up a Sharpie and more Baggies than a second grader's momma needs. I drew a line on my foot so I'd have something to aim for. I want to take off about a third of my foot at an angle. I'll lose three toes but should be able to keep everything from the arch back to the heel. The problem is that it's my left foot that's crushed—on the outside—and I'm right-handed.

I've got to strike fast and strike hard, hopefully hitting in the right place and doing everything in one go, because oxy or not I don't know if I'm going to be able to take another chop after the first one. I pick up the flint, adjust it in my hand so that it feels right, and turn my foot inward. It's awkward as hell, and I've never felt so lonely, but I'm the one that's going to die, and there's no one here to stop that from happening but me.

"So fuck it," I say to Davey's hat, and I strike.

Something rolls across the floor, and my first thought is that I missed entirely and dropped the flint, and my second thought is that this camper is sure as hell not set plumb because it rolled pretty far. Then I see it's my foot that's gotten away from me, all the way down to the door, and the flint is sticking up out of the linoleum, stone teeth buried deep.

Then I start bleeding.

It took a second, like my brain had to catch up with

what was happening and tell my veins to bleed, but once they get the message they take it seriously. Blood's everywhere, and I'm trying to ignore how quick it's spreading, like it was just me on the floor and then before I could blink there's me and half my blood down here too.

I don't have time to be scared. I don't get to.

Because I'm only half-done.

I grab the whiskey, glass slick against my bloodied fingers, and before I lose my nerve I upend it over my foot.

I thought I knew pain. Thought that after years of getting cut and punched a few times and falling out of trees and once getting backed over by a cousin's Chevy and breaking my collarbone that I knew what it was to hurt.

I didn't know shit.

All those pains were familiar, things I'd already experienced that I could file away as something I lived through. A burn, a bruise, a solid smack in the head that left me dizzy for days one time when a scree went out from under me and I landed on rocks. Even though they hurt I could put any of those up against something that came before, compare it and say I made it once, I'll make it again.

This I don't know. This is everything I have inside of me singing at a pitch that'll break your eardrum. This is life-changing pain. This is why animals kick.

I've seen it often. A rabbit in a hawk's claws, a mouse in a cat's death grip, a dog that got clocked by the driver in front of me, and the groundhog that I shot because he kept coming into my 4-H garden. They all kick, a reaction to the pain like maybe they're still trying to run because all they want is to get away from the hurt.

I'm kicking too, my good foot going right through a cupboard door and sending pill bottles everywhere. I kick and I kick and it doesn't help, but I keep doing it anyway because it's all I know. I don't even have sounds, just air in my throat that I can't pull in or push out because I've stopped breathing, and then it does come, all in a rush, every sound I've kept inside of me since I found Duke with Natalie and my friends left me behind, all of it rushes out, and I swear it could lift the roof right off this thing but it doesn't. And I'm screaming and I'm kicking and my good foot is scissoring through my own blood, and I keep hoping I'll pass out, but I don't.

Because I was born with teeth and fingernails, and both of those were made for hanging on.

Davey Beet told me once to call for him if I got lost.

So I try it.

I call for him again and again, losing volume as I go,

his hat a filthy ball in my hands that I've been kneading at in my pain. I move on from Davey to my dad, and I even try God and Jesus, but nobody shows.

There's nobody here but me, so I've got to sit up and do what needs to be done. I get onto my elbows and let the wave of black in my vision settle before going the rest of the way up, leaning forward to see what's left of my foot.

Somehow, someway, I got it just right.

Everything's cut off clean as a whistle. I take what's left of my shirt and soak it in whiskey, then bandage my foot. It burns again, bright and sharp, but I've already been through it and know what to expect. I take a deep breath and lie back for a minute until it passes. Then I undo the tourniquet and watch the bandage soak through with blood.

I'm fading fast, so I take another oxy and a swig of whiskey, followed by water. I got it into my head that maybe if I drink enough the alcohol will chase the infection right out of my veins. I doubt that's good medical advice, but I also don't give much of a shit as I crawl through my own blood to the mattress. All I want is sleep, and the comfort of my moldy blanket.

A patch of sun is coming through the window onto the mattress. I lay in it, my head fuzzy and the pain very much still there but somehow less important than it was a minute before. I don't know if I'm dying or getting better, but I do know that I put Davey Beet's hat back on, so I put my hands on both sides of my head and curl into a ball.

There's no kick left in me.

I am a dying animal, alone in the sun.

I am the deer skull I found forever ago, beside the trail.

I am so very tired.

My limbs are concrete and the mattress water; I feel as if I'm sinking into it. Either that or I'm water and the mattress is solid, because every time I shift it's like the movement keeps on going even once my body stops, the bed the only thing keeping me from becoming pure liquid and dripping right out the door.

Like water I'd search for a low point, slipping down the ridge and into the little stream at the bottom, joining a creek and then a river. I'd slide past my hometown and maybe see Duke fishing off the bridge, and then I'd go on out to sea, all my pain and everything, until I am a single drop in the ocean.

I'm not okay and I know it, but there's a sense of calm in being high, like all my troubles are balloons floating just above me and now that I'm awake enough I can pull them down one at a time for examination.

First there's the pain, a shiny red balloon full to

bursting. The oxy didn't make it go away, for sure. I can still feel it, hot and bright, but it's not the first thing on my mind. It's someone else's problem, a confidence whispered by a friend that made me feel bad for them but left behind in a rush when I take off for a run. My pain is something to be remembered later, when it occurs to me.

Duke is a blue balloon, half-deflated, hovering somewhere over my face like a moth that can't decide whether to land in the fire. Now that I'm not worried about dying—not that it won't happen, I'm just not worried about it anymore—I can't stop thinking about him and Natalie, the sound he made that I thought was for my ears alone.

Exposed bone and sliced nerves I can ignore, but even the oxy can't touch how it feels when I remember finding them. It hurts. More than taking off a piece of my own body, even. I wave that balloon away, not able to deal with it yet. My hand keeps going, all coordination lost, and bounces off the side of the camper to fall back across my face. Davey's hat is scratchy against my wrist and soaked with sweat. I pull it off but keep it nearby, convinced that I smell a bit of him in it.

There's a white balloon up there too, one with a string so long I didn't notice it until I moved. It's up against the roof, so high above me I can't imagine what problem

I've got that it could be so far from me and still cause issues.

Then I realize it's my momma.

She wrote me a letter once. Dad kept it for a few weeks, debating about whether to give it to me. It wasn't him that made the decision but a raccoon that snuck into the trailer and trashed the place, leaving bits of dinner, his own shit, and pieces of our mail everywhere. I found the letter from Mom in the kitchen sink next to a chewed chunk of Colby cheese he'd drug out of the trash and a half-full can of beer (I don't know if Dad drank that or the coon did).

Momma told me in her letter that she wished she could say that leaving me was the hardest thing she ever did, but it wasn't. She said it was an easy decision, because I didn't need her. Dad did, she said—maybe too much. And leaving him wasn't that hard of a call because you get tired of picking up a grown man's socks, but whenever she tried to brush my hair for me I just yelped and told her to leave me alone.

She said she always wanted a girl, but what she got was me.

I didn't know what to make of that, so I folded it up and kept it under my pillow for a while, looking at her writing to see if there were any of her whirls and loops in mine. But there wasn't. My letters were all hard angles and dark slashes, like Dad's, and who cares if there's socks on the floor, anyway?

Maybe I didn't need her brushing my hair, but I guess I could've used a word of advice a time or two, like the first few times I got into fights with Duke, or even when things were going really well. Maybe even more then, come to think of it. She thought I didn't need her, but I needed something more than just Duke's mom reminding him to wear a condom. At least I had that though. She didn't want him to get straddled with kids before twenty, but it would've been my ass too, and maybe she didn't want to see me living somewhere with a nice-enough basement but a man who came home and made everything quieter than church.

Not that Duke would act like that, but he would take another girl into the woods, which is a whole different kind of problem, and maybe if I had a mom I could go home and talk to about it I would've done exactly that instead of punching him in the face and running into the woods, drunk, ending up with half a foot and high on oxy in an old meth lab wearing a dead boy's hat and wrapped in a moldy blanket.

And the worst part is, I consider this an improvement.

DAY SIX

The dead bit of my foot is rotting by the door. It's getting warmer, and the camper works like an oven, my foot a bad piece of meat, cooking slow in the heat.

I wake to the smell, sunlight slanted at an angle that tells me it's late afternoon, and my tongue so dry it's swollen. The flask sits on the floor where I left it, miraculously intact after my kicking fit. I sit up slowly, deciding if I'm drunk, high, or coming down from both. It must be the last because even though I'm woozy my foot hurts like shit set on fire. I unwrap the bandage to have a look.

I'm swelled still, but the red lines of infection might be retreating. I tilt my foot in the sunlight, trying to gauge if that's true or if I've suddenly decided to be an

optimist. But I think I'm right, and somehow the swelling looks less angry, which I know is hardly a medical
term but is somehow completely accurate.

I slide to the edge of the mattress, good foot first,
and put my heel down in my own blood, now tacky and
drying. The floor is covered, and it sticks to me like
syrup as I get down on my butt, scooting over to the
flask and the one granola bar I've got left. I crawl past
the piece of flint, still stuck into the linoleum like a
tombstone for my foot.

My foot thumps like my heart decided to vacate my
chest and move down there, so I lean against the wall,
propping it onto the counter and wiping my hands as
clean as possible on my jeans. I swig back what's left of
the water even though it's flat and stale, and try to figure out how long I can afford to stay here.

I don't know whose setup this is, but I do know that
nobody stays away from this many pills for long. Judging by how my uncle Chuck was dealt with for making
junk meth on the side, I don't think the owner of this
camper will take kindly to me knowing where their stash
is kept, or kicking in their door, for that matter.

I'm a girl alone where she doesn't belong, and one
who will be presumed dead in a week or so. If someone
were to finish off that process a little more quickly than
nature intends and dump my body elsewhere, nobody

would think anything of it—and that's if I ever got found in the first place.

The pill bottles are still strewn across the floor and I reach for one, feeling a little tug of resistance as my dried blood tries to keep it. The label's been torn off to hide who it was stolen from, but the date it was filled is still up in the corner. I count backward and figure out that it was filled maybe ten days ago, which means somewhere between then and now it got up to a ridge in the woods and somebody is going to be coming back sooner or later to fill all these little sandwich Baggies with something that doesn't belong between two slices of bread.

I rest my head against the wall, rolling the bottle back and forth across my palm and shifting my foot on the counter. There's a chance that the person who comes up here to count pills is decent, like my uncle. Just someone who needed to make a buck and cashed in on the only industry we've got left. They might give me the shirt off their back—literally—to cover my nakedness, draw me fresh water and other biblical stuff and then take me to the ER, which isn't so Jesusy but would be a lot more helpful.

They might.

Or they might drag me out of here screaming, beat what's left of me into a pulp so that only my dental records can identify me, or not worry about anybody ever finding me and end it quick with a bullet to the head. I run my tongue over my teeth at the thought, dislodging the last crumbs of granola. I don't know how long I've been here, but I do know I'll leave on my own accord and not one drop of my blood spilled that I didn't shed myself.

I also can't live on meth and whiskey, the only things they seem to store out here. Wherever I am is a far piece from anything else, and food won't find me. I've got to go to it. Might as well be headed toward something while looking for food, rather than waiting for a drug dealer to show up and hoping he won't kill me and brought more granola.

"One more day," I say into the hot, close air of the camper. "You get one more day."

I find my dead bit of foot and put it in a sandwich bag.

There's a weird comfort in having all of me back in one place as I crawl onto the mattress. I've got an oxy in one hand and the bag in the other; I dry-swallow the first and hold the second close to my chest.

There's a small TV in the corner, sitting precariously on a shelf that wasn't built to hold that kind of weight. It's the only kind of TV I've ever had, the heavy ones with so much ass on them you've got to wrap your arms around them to pick them up. No flat-screens in my family, no sir.

The screen can't show anything but a reflection now, the slats of the blinds and the moonlight coming in. Makes me think about being out with Meredith and Kavita one night, driving around looking for a field party. Jason and Duke were supposed to meet us at the gas station, but Uncle Chuck said they'd already come and gone and neither one of them was answering their phones, so we headed out to the back roads to find them ourselves.

There were three different places we got together for drinking, an old abandoned barn out on 149, under the bridge that the county closed a couple of years ago, and—if it was a hot summer—the dried-up creek bed on the low side of the dam. We didn't find the boys or anyone else at any of the usual spots, so we ended up just cruising with nothing to do and nowhere to go.

Until I spotted a TV in the ditch. I made Meredith stop and carried it back to the car, cutting my hand on the cracked screen when I put it in the back seat beside Kavita who was working on a bottle of peppermint schnapps. I was pissed at Duke and Jason for leaving us behind and not answering their phones, angry at the person who threw anything they didn't want in a ditch,

and ready to kill over the fact that their trash was something I couldn't have afforded in a month of Sundays. I
had Meredith drive us back to the gas station and asked
Uncle Chuck if I could put a TV in their dumpster. He
didn't seem at all fazed by that.

"Sure," he said, eyeing me and Kavita over the rolls
of lottery tickets. "By the way you're bleeding and your
friend smells like a candy cane."

He took an ACE bandage off the shelf for my hand
and gave Kavita a stick of gum and told us both to go
home before we got pulled over. She helped me heave
the flat-screen into the trash, the broken pieces of a
hundred beer bottles grinding under our feet as we did.
When we got back into the car Meredith snapped off
the music.

"I think I saw a microwave down by the creek out on
Twenty-Eight," she said.

And that's how I ended up drunk and wandering
around the countryside with a car full of busted-up
housewares. By the end we had that microwave, a blender,
the footboard of a child's bed, two alarm clocks, and a
lamp that still worked but needed a shade. We went back
to Meredith's, and she found one in her attic and draped
a scarf over it while Kavita poured more schnapps. Duke
texted around one in the morning to see if we wanted to

hang out, and I took a selfie of the three of us, snock-
ered, with middle fingers in the air, that lamp lighting
up the room.

It was the background on my phone for the longest
time—me, my friends, and the ditch lamp. In it I've got
a bandage around my hand from the cut I got on the
TV, and if I looked at my palm right now I could still
see the scar.

But I can't.

I can't open my hand and I can't turn my head and I
don't even know if my eyes are shut or not. Everything is
slippery again, and I think the balloons are back, especially the red one, filled near to busting and tempting
me to swat at it so it can break, raining all the pain
down on me.

The blue and the white are there too, and now that I
think about it I guess maybe there are more than that,
even. Like someone brought me a whole bunch of balloons and they thought it was a gift but all it really does
is make me think of something I've done wrong for each
one, or somebody I hurt.

My mom's up there still, and Duke. But so's Dad from
that time I blamed him for her leaving. Meredith and
Kavita are here too, I can feel them hovering, reminding
me of every time I made Meredith feel dumb, or disappointed Kavita by not being a better person. There's a

whole cloud of bad hovering over me, and all I can do is pull Davey Beet's hat down tighter over my head.

Even though everyone I'm thinking about makes me feel bad one way or another, I'd give anything to have one of them here with me right now. So I do the only thing I can think of and start calling for them. I yell for my mom and my dad, Meredith and Kavita, Davey Beet and Jesus, too. I call for Duke, in the end, because Jesus is all about love and forgiveness, and while that's nice, what I really need is someone with basic first aid training and enough muscle mass to carry me out of here.

When I'm done yelling, I cry.

DAY SEVEN

I open my eyes, and the first thing I think is, *This is the day that the Lord has made,* followed by the answer, *Let us rejoice and be glad in it.*

It's so funny I could puke, but there's nothing in my stomach.

They taught us all kinds of stuff at Camp Little Fish, but that one kind of stuck, mostly because I was the only camper there on what they called a *scholarship* instead of *charity*. But the other kids would say this, eyes big and bright over breakfast, like maybe they were happy about something I didn't understand.

I still don't understand.

What I can say is that while I'm not exactly glad right now, and rejoicing is off the table, I also don't feel like

I'm dying. I sit up, expecting a wave of blackness in my vision or a revolt in my gut, but I get neither. I'm light-headed and weak, with nothing but opioids and alcohol in my system. I'm still in a camper with more of my blood on the floor than inside me, and part of my body in a sandwich bag, but weirdly, I feel okay.

"Huh," I say, which is the best kind of thanks I can manage right now.

What's left of my foot looks better, the red lines receding for sure. The bleeding has stopped, and the flesh from where I amputated looks healthy and pink. The bone nubs sticking out are cut cleanly, a small miracle.

I start unraveling Davey Beet's hat.

I don't want to, and it hurts my heart more than a little when I pick out the knot at the crown that his mom tucked in when she finished it. I pull it through and bite it off, the yarn coming loose and free, tightly kinked from years of being a hat, soaked in rain, snow, Davey's sweat, and my tears. I take it down about an inch, which gives me a decent length of yarn. I bite it off again, retying a knot and putting Davey's hat back on, the top of my head now poking through it.

I slip a sandwich bag over my hurt foot and push open the door to the camper.

It's a beautiful day, and I could almost rejoice and be

glad in it if I had more than dandelions to eat. I chew
for a bit before I swallow, like a cow with cud. Making
my way down to the water isn't easy, but I manage, the
Erlenmeyer flask bumping against my side from where
I tied it to my belt loop with a bit of yarn. I fill it up at
the stream, drink good, and fill it again.

I strip down and clean myself as best I can, my clothes
too. I'm resting on the bank, stark naked, the sun warm-
ing me and actually feeling a little decent.

Nice things haven't been all that easy to come by
in my life, but I do have one or two good memories,
like the time a lifeguard taught me to swim at the public pool, or when I was ten and Duke's older brother,
Wayne, kicked the shit out of a sixth grader for trying
to pull me under the tube slide for a kiss during recess.
I took another oxy before I came down to the water,
and I'm all messed-up again in my head, every thought
seems connected to the next, cascading one to the other
without pause. It's like pulling weeds after a good rain,
each one bringing up more earth than you bargained for
and leaving a hole behind.

Wayne showed me how to make a fist that day on the
playground and offered to let me throw a punch at him
just so I'd know how it feels. I took him up on it, and he
walked away with a bloody mouth, but he was smiling,
and it was probably the best recess I ever had.

I wonder what he'd think now that I used the same fist to break his brother's nose, whether he'd tell me I lost my shit or offer to hold Duke while I took a second shot. There it is now, and I can't ignore it. I pulled on that particular weed and it came up, root system and all, and I've got a big, gaping hole to stare at and figure out what I'm going to fill it with.

I've got two options, forgiveness or anger. I can't act like I don't care, the way Kavita has always been able to do about Jason. Something inside of me burns too strong and too deep. It doesn't help that everything I feel shows on my face. Meredith's always been better at making her face do what it's supposed to, so maybe it's her that should've been teaching me things on the playground instead of Wayne.

I don't know, but I've still got this hole to consider, and I can just about do what Davey Beet and Jesus and everyone at Camp Little Fish wants me to do, which is forgive Duke for cheating on me. Then I think about those words—*cheated on me*—and I get angry again, my gut burning hotter than my foot.

When I found him with Natalie it felt like neither one of us could do anything other than cry, but I've had time to think, and I've got words to say now, lots of them. Some are bad and most are mean, but the one that keeps popping up and wants to be said is *why?*

Why'd he have to go and do that?

Why wasn't I enough?

Why can't a nice thing stay that way?

When his brother Wayne got shot in the ass for banging Kate Fullerton, we all laughed about it. Wayne was laid out on the sofa in the front room with a bandage on his ass, a bottle of whiskey going between him, me, and Duke. Wayne was telling it like it was a funny story, not like he'd just been shot and warned off a girl he'd been in love with. I was laughing because I thought I was supposed to, the whole time thinking, *How is this the same guy who punched a boy for trying to kiss me?*

Maybe time changed Wayne. Or maybe all boys are one way to their girls and a different way with everyone else. Maybe Duke tells stories about me to other guys when I'm not around. Maybe seeing Natalie made him remember how they had a nice thing going too, until he passed her up for me. Maybe I didn't know him as well as I thought, or maybe he heard me say Davey Beet's name one too many times.

I don't know.

One thing I do know is that Kate Fullerton got a dog out of that whole mess. Her family said she had some kind of stress disorder after seeing her dad put a load of shot into Wayne's ass, and insurance paid for her to get a therapy dog. She took it to school and everything, and got to pet it whenever she was feeling sad, and all I could think was I'd wanted a dog my whole life and we never could afford one.

Maybe I'll get a therapy dog out of this whole mess.

Good thing I don't have one now though, 'cause I'd eat it.

When Kavita moved here from the suburbs she didn't understand about hunting. She thought it was about killing things, so I showed her otherwise. When I invited her to come with me she'd given me a funny kind of side-eye but must've thought it was something like a dare, so she agreed. I got an even funnier look when we started hiking out to the woods and I didn't have a gun.

"You're fast," she said. "But you can't tell me you're going to run down a deer and kill it with your bare hands."

I just gave her a smile, and she seemed to think about it for a second and then added, "Then again, maybe it wouldn't be all that surprising."

I helped Kavita up into the stand I had in the woods, then settled myself into Duke's, up in a tree a few yards away. Then we did the hard part of hunting, together.

"So what's going on?" she asked me after maybe five minutes. "What are we doing out here?"

"Hunting," I told her. "This is the part where you

wait, and you watch. I don't take a gun with me until I know there'll be something to shoot at. And I only shoot at something I'm going to eat."

She came out with me three more times, until I'd spotted the deer I wanted. I don't trophy hunt; we can't afford to taxidermy anything, so I kill for meat and not antlers. I found a doe I liked and let her know which one it would be. Kavita didn't come with me the next time, and I get that.

Watching things die isn't easy.

Neither is killing them.

I don't have days to wait and watch and plan. I told myself I was putting some distance between me and the camper in the morning, and I will. But there's got to be something more in my stomach than plants if I'm going to have the strength to do it. I don't know these woods, or the paths these animals take. I can't go to them, so instead I've got to bring them to me.

I've only got one thing to lure them with, and that's my own rotting foot.

I find a good clearing not too far from the camper just as the sun was going down, a chill rising in the air. I toss the bit of foot out of my bag and settle in nearby, hoping it's something small that comes. Something I can clobber with my walking stick.

It's a possum that shows up, of course, its long

snakelike tail switching back and forth as it scents the air. I got lucky, and it came into the clearing from upwind, the smell of the lure way stronger than anything I'm giving off. It settles in, snacking on my toes like it's a bag of chips, and while I'm thrilled my plan is working I didn't prep myself for watching something eat my foot.

I'm all right when it takes an experimental bite. I even hang in there when it pulls off a shred of my skin. It's the snap of my bone cracking underneath its teeth that sends me across the clearing, walking stick in hand, ready to bash its brains in. I move as fast as I can, swinging wide as soon as the possum is in reach. I get it in the side and it goes sprawling, spitting out one of my toes and a surprised bark along with it.

I'm screwed because I missed what I was aiming for—the head. It's not stunned, and it's going to bolt, the caterwaul it just made scaring off anything else that might have been coming to investigate. Everything's lost, and I just fed my foot to a wild animal for no good reason because it got what it came for and now it's going to make a run for it. But it doesn't. Instead, the possum gets up and rounds on me, back up, showing its teeth.

That's when I spot the babies.

They're lined up at the edge of the clearing, waiting for the momma's permission to come in and have some of what she found. Then I showed up and whacked her a good one, and she's going to fight me rather than run and leave her babies behind.

It's so goddamn sad I can't take it.

But I also can't die out here, so I'm crying when I take the next swing, right on the side of her skull. The momma goes flying, still spitting and doing her best to keep my attention on her and leave her babies alone. She gets back up, coming at me with what she's got left, and I cave in her head with a last thump that should send her babies running but they don't.

They stand there, looking at me.

I just killed their momma right in front of them, and they're so young they don't even know to run from me. I'm the scariest thing they'll ever see in their life, a wild woman with their momma's blood spattered on her face, and all they can do is stare at me, shocked.

But there's another part of me that knows they're an easy kill, and fresh meat.

"Get out of here," I scream before I change my mind. I drop my stick and charge, so that they scatter, their tails the last thing I see as they disappear into the night. I taught them that there's nothing worse than humans. And while I learned it young myself, I didn't ever want to have to be the one bearing the message.

I grab my kill and, after a second of thought, pick up

what's left of my foot and stick it in the bag. I can't give a good reason other than I keep thinking about the deer skull I found by the trail on the way in, flesh long since rotted into the ground underneath. I love the woods, more than a roof over my head.

But damn if it can have me, even a little bit.

I tear some tin off the side of the camper, careful not to slice a finger off in the process. My fire starts easy, another burn hole added to my fireboard. I strike off a piece of flint with a good edge and skin the possum, taking away every last thing that will cook up. The meat sizzles on the tin as it warms next to the fire, and in all my life I have never smelled anything so wonderful.

I have meat, and it helps with the guilt. Taking down a deer was never easy for me, but knowing that it would get us through the winter without having to pay for grocery meat was what made my finger pull the trigger. The methodical business of butchering takes concentration, and busy hands don't allow for an idle mind. I don't think of the motherless babies in the woods when I take my first bite of real food in a week. All I think is how damn good it is to eat again.

I take it slow, letting the pain pass in my stomach and the business of digestion begin before I eat a second strip of meat, my foot resting on the steps of the camper. The sun is edging into the sky by the time I've cooked up everything and sealed it all away in Baggies, making a tiny hole above the sealing line with the tip of my flint and stringing yarn through them.

It's time to go, and I'm ready.

I've scoured around the trailer looking for any sign, a hint of a trail they use to come and go, but there's nothing. A smart person would come a different way every time, letting new growth fill in what they trampled. A really smart person would leave by a different route, too, and I seem to have crossed paths with the smartest drug dealer in the county, as luck would have it. I think of Uncle Chuck, beaten unconscious beside his burned-out trailer, a harsh warning to leave off what he was doing.

There's a chance whoever's setup this is ended up the same—or worse off. Or maybe they sampled too much of their own product and their return is permanently delayed, the woods filling in all the signs of their passage. Or maybe I've been enjoying the hospitality of the same person who smashed in Chuck's face and won't take too kindly to me drinking all their whiskey.

I just don't know.

I pocket three oxys—enough to take the edge off if I need it in the coming days, but not to the point of making me funny in the head. The whiskey is gone, so I rinse out the bottle and thread yarn through the handle, tying it through a belt loop on my jeans. I'm still lame enough to need the walking stick and can't carry the blanket easily, so I tie the edges around my neck, a moldy cape. I tuck the slice of flint into my waistband and get my bad foot back into the sling.

I put what's left of the possum on the meth lab counter to rot.

Because fuck them.

DAY EIGHT

Today I'm going to walk until I see something left behind by another human being.

I can't set a distance goal because each step takes as much energy as a mile would on a normal day. My body is taking a beating that makes me feel like I'm covering more distance than I am, but when I take an oxy for the pain, everything gets fuzzy. Not just the pain, but also time and any sense of the distance that I've covered.

So instead I say I'm going to move until I find evidence of someone else, something to tell me that I'm close enough to civilization that a person has passed through. Even if it's litter tossed aside from whoever is operating out of that camper, at least I'll know I'm following in their footsteps, and those will lead me out of the woods.

Unnatural things always turned my gut a bit, like the plastic wrappers I'd find alongside the trail or a ball of fishing line left behind in a tangle that couldn't be undone. But I'd give my good foot to see something that means another person was out here not too long ago, or a flash of neon from a power walker that would lead me to the trail.

Right now, I'm the foreign object, the trespasser, everything from the elastic in my bra to the Baggies hanging from my belt loops declaring me unnatural. My mind has been wandering, maybe because my legs aren't doing a great job of it themselves. The meat is helping, but I'm not in fighting shape, and my foot feels like I stuck it in a blender, then an oven.

I stop again, take my foot out of the sling, and slide the sandwich bag off to inspect it. It's still puffed up like a cat taking on a pack of dogs, but the redness is gone. I pull open a bag and eat some more possum, well aware that what I've got will go bad in a few days. I eat everything in that pouch and wash it down with whiskey-tinged water.

I'm two shuffling steps away from the big beech I was leaning on when I turn to check that I didn't leave anything behind, because damn if I'm going to be the only person out here and a litterer. And there, right above where I'd been sitting, is the proof I'd been looking for that another human being passed this way, etched into the bark of the tree.

DAVEY BEET WAS HERE

I saw Davey Beet before he went missing.

We ran into each other at the gas station. He was going out as I was coming in and held the door for me, then did a double take when he recognized me. I'd been too terrified to say a word, but when I heard a tentative "Ass-kicker?" I turned around quicker than a weather-vane in a storm.

I was fifteen then, had just gotten my permit and took any excuse to drive, like running into the gas station for a gallon of milk even though there was at least two inches left in the one we had. Davey was twenty, three months from disappearing, and working for a landscaping company. He was tan and fit, hair a little long and curling from underneath his baseball hat.

I could tell he didn't quite know what to think of me, or where to look. My body had filled out that summer, and Meredith had taught me what to wear to show it off. It wasn't so bad that Dad wouldn't let me leave the house, but my cleavage cast a shadow, and I had legs up to my shoulder blades. I hadn't minded the attention I was getting, but I hadn't *liked* it until that moment.

"Hey, Davey," I said, leaving behind the blast of air-conditioning from the gas station and letting the door swing shut behind me. "What've you been up to?"

Not much, it turned out, but all of it was still fascinating because it happened to Davey Beet, and because it was him standing there telling me about it like maybe he was trying to impress me, just a little bit.

"So what's up with you?" he asked, and I told him about getting my permit, kind of leaning hard on the fact that I could go anywhere I wanted now and didn't have a curfew. Technically I was supposed to have an adult in the car with me, but I didn't know too many of those, and Dad was pulling double shifts.

Davey kept nodding, and I don't think I'm flattering myself to say that there was a pause when I think maybe he was going to ask me for my number or see if I wanted to hang out sometime. I was holding my breath, heat coming back up off the asphalt and baking me, mouth drier than it's ever been, even now.

Maybe Davey did the math in that moment, remembered I was only fifteen. Davey Beet was being a good guy when he let that moment pass, and damn if I didn't wish he would've gone ahead and been questionable, just that one time.

His buddy yelled at him from the landscaping truck, and he said it was nice talking to me but he better get back to work, and then Davey walked away, turning back to say something I've carried with me forever.

"You did a good job growing up, Ass-kicker," he called.

I didn't know what to say, so I just nodded. Maybe if I'd been a little older or surer of myself I would've asked him out instead of waiting for him to ask me. Maybe he would've said, "No, but call me when you're eighteen." Maybe that little bit of something I saw in his eyes might've grown into something else, and maybe he wouldn't have gone into the woods when another girl broke his heart.

And maybe I wouldn't be standing here right now, staring at words written by someone who never came back, and was never found.

I go until I can't go no more.

It's not pain or hunger that stops me but pure exhaustion. There's nothing left inside of me but tired when I fall under a big maple and can't get back up again. I lie still, slipping my foot out of the sling and rolling onto my back so that I can look up at the canopy, and the bits of darkening sky in between.

It's evening. Frogs are singing, and the light has that special kind of tint to it that used to make me want to go outside and stay there, which is pretty funny to me now. I might've left Davey Beet's name behind me on that tree, but it's burned onto my eyes, and all I can think about as I stare is that my mind has spent so much time thinking about Davey that now, somehow, I'm following him.

It's a crazy thought, and yes, I did pop an oxy when I refilled my whiskey bottle at the last bit of running water I found, but I'm not sure it wouldn't have occurred to me even without the drugs. Davey's always been a safe place to return to, a what-if that kept me going through bad fights with Duke, or rough patches at home, like the time I told Dad that maybe if we didn't live in a trailer I'd bring my friends over more often.

I'm embarrassed thinking about that, even out here.

It's one of those moments that'll dog me the rest of my life, like the first time I was invited to a birthday party and was the only kid who showed up without a present, or when Kate Fullerton recognized the shirt I was wearing because it used to be hers and she gave it to the Goodwill. Shame burns over time, leaving behind a scar that puckers up and shines so that it can't ever be quite forgotten.

It happened after I started driving and Dad made the comment that I'd been making myself so scarce that he might start calling me Wendy (my momma's name), and I don't know if it was his timing or the fact that it was just a bad thing to say to a motherless girl, but I lit into him like it was Fourth of July and he had a fuse sticking out.

I told him maybe I'd stay home more if there was something better to eat other than venison and mac and cheese. I said maybe I'd spend more time with him if we actually played catch instead of just watching baseball on the TV, or maybe I'd even bring my friends over to our place instead of going to theirs if it didn't risk them seeing him running around in his tighty-whities, beer gut hanging out over them while he made the trip to the fridge for the next one.

I said all those things to the person who raised me, the parent who stayed, the one who fed me and dressed me and read me books every night and made high-pitched voices for the girl characters. And every word I said cut him deep, down through skin and bone and biting into the soul. I watched it happen, and I kept going, saying all the bad things I could think of until he shoved open the screen door and told me to leave if things were so bad. But he cracked it open so hard it snapped right off in his hand, leaving him holding a door with no hinges, owner of a house with no proper entrance.

His face just kinda fell, like the world had ganged up on him in the form of his daughter and his own home. I was pissed too, at our trailer for being so shitty, at the door for falling off right then, even if all it did was prove my point. I didn't need fate on my side to illustrate how bad off we were, so I took the door and threw it out in the front yard and stomped on it until my feet went through the screen and the metal frame was bent to hell.

It wasn't the smartest thing I ever did, but it felt good. And after that Dad and I went to the hardware store and got a new door and put it on together and had some beer and watched a ball game. We didn't talk about the fight, just slipped into our old routines and did them like always, working together without saying much, knowing what the other was going to do, or what tool they needed without words.

Dad and I were always like that, not needing to talk to communicate. As I watch the light fade out of the sky, I wonder if he could hear me right now if I told him that I love him and that I'm sorry about all that and about all this too. I wonder if he's watching a baseball game right now, or how many beers he's had, or if the door is slapping in the wind that's kicking up because he managed to fuck up the whole doorframe when he tore it off.

The truth is I miss my shitty house, and not just for the shelter.

It is home, and has someone in it who loves me.

I tried going to church for a bit.

The memories get into my head because I'm looking up at the maple branches and there's a spot where one overlaps another and damn if I didn't lie down with a cross right above my head.

Dad always said there were enough people in his life asking him to be grateful for this or that, and forgiveness didn't come easy when his days were mostly filled with people doing him wrong, like the guy who took his overtime shift when we were in the kind of tight spot that meant the electric might get turned off. But he didn't care if I went, and Camp Little Fish was associated with some sort of Methodist group, so I ended up displaying enough interest the second summer I was there to get involved in a carpool.

There was a nice lady that came to get me every Sunday morning, her own kids in the back with their shirts buttoned up and their nylons tight on their legs like sausage skins. I didn't have anything of the sort, so I just wore clean jeans and a T-shirt that didn't have bad words on it, and nobody seemed to think sideways of it. True, people from church did start giving me bags of clothes, along with casual comments like it was spring-cleaning time, or it didn't fit their daughter anymore and would save them the bother of doing a garage sale if I took it.

I didn't mind so much because they weren't ever giving me silly dresses or stuff that I couldn't get good wear out of. One guy even gave me what he claimed was his son's old hiking boots, but if they were used then his son never set foot outside because they smelled like fresh rubber and fit snug like they just came out of a box. The people there were nice enough, and I never once felt talked down to or lorded over.

It's funny to think about having too much pride when you're gnawing on a possum leg, but maybe that's what my issue was, in the end. Because after a while I started to feel the weight of those clothes on my back, every friendship I made a debt that was owed. Also, I tried to put on a pair of pantyhose and it didn't go too well.

Someone gave me a pair, along with a jean skirt that I figured I could wear without feeling too awkward, since it was denim after all. But the pantyhose were giving me problems that morning. I'd never had a pair on in my life and didn't know a thing about all the pinching and pulling and shimmying; Meredith taught me those things later. At that time, I was twelve and thought everything worked like cotton undies or jeans, you just stepped in and pulled up.

That theory was failing me, and the nylons were winning the battle when I lost my balance and pitched over in the tiny bathroom of our trailer, smacking my face against the wall and getting the edge of the towel rod jammed into my hip. I said a word my ride wouldn't have approved of and glanced out the window to see her pulling in. I couldn't go without the hose because I didn't have any clean underwear, Dad was snoring away in his room and wouldn't have been any help anyway, not for pantyhose.

So I kept pulling and pulling and put my fingers right through the damn things, sending a runner from hip to toenail. My ride tapped the horn—once, politely—and I said another bad word, although I admit that one might have been directed at her and not my clothing. At that point I was crying with frustration and didn't know what to do. I was too embarrassed to waddle to the door and wave her on, and I couldn't get the damn things off either, so I just sat on the floor in the bathroom, defeated by a piece of women's clothing no one had ever taught me to put on, and waited for my ride to give up and go away.

She did, eventually, but showed up again the next week. I'd been told often enough by both my dad and Jesus that lying was a bad thing, so I didn't have the nerve to tell her I'd been sick and wasn't about to admit to the truth. So I did the easy thing, covered my head with the blanket and waited for her to go away. She was persistent, even coming up to the door by the end of the month but going away in a hurry when Dad answered in his undies.

Eventually her honking on the horn made the neighbors in the next trailer take a potshot at her with a .22 one morning and that was the final straw. I never went to church again and burned those pantyhose in the barrel out back first chance I got. I can't say I missed it, but there was something that stuck with me.

They were pretty big on Psalm 23, the one about the Lord being your shepherd and making you lie down in green pastures and not being afraid to walk through the valley of the shadow of death, which I admit would be a nice backup to have right about now.

But my eyes always wandered over to Psalm 22 instead. While everyone else was reciting the reassuring stuff, I read about real shit going down, the way my life actually was. I can recite it, even now.

"'Be not far from me,'" I say. "'For trouble is near

and there is no one to help.'"

I don't know if I'm saying it because I think there might actually be a God to listen or if I'm just distracting myself, but I lick the possum grease off my lips and keep going.

"'Roaring lions that tear their prey open their mouths wide against me.'"

That hasn't quite happened yet, but at this rate nothing would be surprising.

"'I am poured out like water, and all my bones are out of joint. My heart has turned to wax; it has melted within me.'"

That last bit of oxy is still swimming in my veins, and while I don't think that's quite what the Bible was talking about when it comes to being poured out like water, it sure does feel similar. My voice quavers when I think about my heart melting within me and the sound Duke made when he took his pleasure with Natalie under the light of the moon.

"'My mouth is dried up like a potsherd, and my tongue sticks to the roof of my mouth; you lay me in the dust of death.'"

The first bit couldn't be truer; I'm hoping the last is just symbolic.

"'Dogs surround me, a pack of villains encircles me; they pierce my hands and my feet.'"

What's left of my feet anyway. I don't know how much more piercing I can take.

"'All my bones are on display; people stare and gloat over me.'"

That's truer than I care to admit, but if there were anyone to stare, my situation would be a lot better off and I'd let them go ahead and gloat.

"'They divide my clothes among them and cast lots for my garment.'"

Between all the strips torn off my shirt I went ahead and did the dividing myself, and anybody is welcome to my jeans if they drive me to the hospital first.

"'But you, LORD, be not far from me. You are my strength; come quickly to help me.'"

The sooner the better.

DAY NINE

I put away what's left of the possum in the morning, afraid it'll go bad if I wait much longer. It goes down easy, my stomach understanding its purpose. I know this means I'll be in that much more pain if I begin the process of starving again, but I can only hope that's not in store for me.

I stick my empty Baggies in one pocket and the one with something left in it—one oxy—in the other. My bad foot is still swollen, but the wound looks as clean as I can expect it to. I put some plastic over it and pop it back in the sling, adjust my walking stick under my armpit and set out once more.

I keep thinking there's got to be an end to this, that we've obliterated so much of our natural habitat that sooner or later I'm going to stumble across a road, an ATV trail, a natural-gas operation . . . something. People have never been decent about leaving nature alone, tearing into her with machines of metal teeth and money-hungry mouths. How many times did I have to pull to the side to let a gas truck pass me, the little road that led to my house too small for the both of us?

A lot, that's how many. And I cussed them every time, getting to the point where I think the guys got a kick out of me giving them the finger and started using my road more often just to see me go off on them from behind the steering wheel. Dad always said if I didn't give people such a reaction they'd stop giving me so much shit.

Still, I'd be all right with seeing a company truck right now. Like maybe I wouldn't even cuss them. But I can't find a walking trail, let alone a road, so I don't see that anywhere in my immediate future.

I stop to fill my whiskey bottle when I hear the ripple of a creek, this one deep enough that it has a decent flow to it and a couple of slow pools near the rocks where I see some smallmouth bass passing the time, their mouths opening and closing in a rhythm that my own breathing picks up, slow and steady. I don't know why I'm thinking so hard out here about all the things I've done wrong. Maybe because I've got nothing but time and I haven't exactly done a whole lot of things right.

Once my bottle is full I climb back up the bank awkwardly, grabbing on to trees and pulling myself with my arms more than I am using my good leg. I lose my balance enough to knock against a little elm, scraping the raw edge of my foot against it and sending a blaze across my brain.

I dig out the oxy and break it in half with my fingernail, although a lot of the nail gets bent back before the pill gives away. I'm malnourished, all the little bits that used to make up *me* draining away, slowly. I get back up, hobbling into position and leaning a touch to the side where the whiskey bottle hangs heavy. I know it's going to pull me as I go. I know I'm nowhere near to making a straight line as I hobble forward, walking stick, then good foot.

But at least I'm still moving.

The best way to spot a trail is to not look right at it.

Anybody that knows the woods gets that, but trying to teach someone how to see things without looking is a tall order. I knew the woods around our house well enough to be aware of the deer paths and raccoon stomping grounds, and Dad taught me how to gauge the size of a deer from its print, but it was Davey Beet that showed me how to find a trail where there were no tracks.

"Right there," he told me, grabbing my wrist right before I went down to the edge of a ravine.

Embarrassed that I fell and even more because he'd caught me, I shook him off. "What's right where?"

Davey nodded to the west, and I'd done what anybody would do, stared hard at the brush, trying to figure out what exactly it was that had his attention.

"Nope," he said. "Don't look at the ground. Look midway up the trees and rest your eyes. Then you'll see it."

And damn if he wasn't right. It was like one of those pictures where a thousand different little things make up one big picture, and if you're looking too close at the details you can't see the overall view.

The deer trail that catches my eye now does so only because I haven't given up scanning the trees for blazes on the off-chance that I'll wander back across the trail. It's not paint that I spot but a knot that either looks like a human face or I've been alone way too long. Whatever the case, I'm looking at that and not the ground when it all comes together, and there's the deer path.

Humans aren't the only creatures of habit. Deer use the same trails, moving from a bedding area to a feeding area to water every day. It's not unusual to find the splayed-finger paws of raccoons and the scratch of a turkey right next to the cloven hoofprint of a deer. A wildlife trail is used often, and by many different types of animals. But that doesn't mean it's screaming for my attention either. Animals move soft and slow through the woods, and spotting a trail means looking for small blades of grass bent the same direction, like how I part my hair when combing it out after a shower.

The path is about as wide as that too and not heading west, but I've been making my own way long enough that it would be nice to follow for a while, so I decide to see what the deer know that I don't. I find a few spots where they've bedded down recently and some scat that tells me they're not far off. There's no real reason why I should care. Like Kavita pointed out a lifetime ago it's not as if I could run one down and kill it with my bare hands. And even if I could, I wouldn't. I couldn't eat a tenth of it and carry about the same before it went bad. It's curiosity that leads me on, not need. So when I come across the fawns I'm not looking them up and down to assess where the good cuts are.

I just enjoy them.

They're grazing in a small clearing, little nubs of teeth pulling up the new grass. They've still got their spots, dazzling white in the sun, contented tails flicking back and forth as they eat. Their mom lifts her head and spots me, falling still and silent. I do the same, waiting for her to snort and let her little ones know that there's a predator nearby and it's time to run.

She doesn't.

That's how I know I'm well and truly fucked.

DAY TEN

My Baggies are empty and so is my stomach.

I didn't bother with a shelter. Instead I crawled in under the low branches of a pine and slept with my fist punched up into my belly like somehow I could trick it into thinking it was full. It didn't work, and I wake up with needles stuck into my skin at odd angles and a grumble in my gut that nothing but food is gonna fix.

It doesn't hurt yet. I've probably got at least two days before I'll be in pain again, so that's something. I pull up some greens and chew on them, rolling them in my mouth same as the deer did the day before, thinking. I still haven't moved out from under the pine when it starts to rain, low-hanging branches keeping me reasonably dry.

I wrap up in my blanket and watch it fall, changing from big, lonely drops into a decent downpour, then becoming a sheet of water. There's nothing I can do but sit, and while I've been telling myself all along to keep moving, like it was a plan that would make everything okay in the end, that motivation is gone.

I try to tell myself that I'm just taking advantage of the little break, that there's no point in wandering around and getting soaked to the skin and sliding down wet ridges and maybe even getting struck by lightning. But the truth is I'm tired. I'm tired of walking and not getting anywhere, tired of everything I've got hurting, right down to my insides. And I'm tired in the sleepy sense too, even though I know I lay down last night before it was fully dark and the sun had already put in half a day's work when I woke.

None of this is good, and I know it.

My body is worn out, and my mind is ready to follow that path. Little things have been happening that I haven't given my full attention to, and now that I'm stuck here I can't quite ignore them anymore. I talked to a tree yesterday, though I don't recall what I said. I know it didn't answer, which is a point in my favor, but the fact that I was disappointed by that is not.

That, and I've been thinking about cheese a lot. I probably put in four miles yesterday and I thought about big orange blocks of Colby the whole time. I can't explain it, but I could see cheese in my mind, right down to the uneven breaks when you pull off a chunk that you want and the way it crumbles in your hand. I even sat down hard at one point, right on my bad foot because it was still up in the sling, and I didn't really think about the pain too much. I was still caught up in cheese.

The color. The smell. The taste. The texture. I even thought about the way the refrigerator gives off a nice *poof* of cold air when you first open it, a prelude to cheese.

"A prelude to cheese," I say to myself aloud. "You're a fucking idiot."

That might be true, but it doesn't mean I can't sit here in the rain, chewing on grass and thinking about cheese. I guess it's because it's something I absolutely can't have. When I was a kid I wanted all kinds of things that I'd never get: a pony, a dog, a mom. So I'd sit around and think about those things, the fun we'd have, how close we'd be, the places we'd go together.

Funny thing is, even in my daydreams I always ended up taking everybody to the woods.

"Ha ha," I say, accidentally losing a piece of greenery from my mouth. I pick it out of my bra and pop it back in.

I curl into a ball, blanket draped over the curve of

my hips—sharper now, I notice. I can count all my ribs, even in the dark, my fingers tripping over them the same way Momma claimed I did to her, but from the inside. My hands wander to my face, tracing the hollows of my eyes, so deep it's like my skull is working its way forward.

I've always known my body, its strength and purpose, the long muscles of my legs and the lean bulge of my biceps. This is different; this is an intimacy with my skeleton, from the exposed broken tips in my foot to the sharp corner of my jaw digging into the ground as I try to get comfortable. I'm learning the deeper parts of me, maybe even past the ones a doctor can name. Right down into my soft bits and then further, where things you can't actually touch live.

I'm discovering me out here, for the good and the bad. There's things I'm proud of and stuff I'd rather forget, but it all makes up who I am and what I was, and what I've got to work with if I want to become something else. And I don't get to do those things or be that person if I die out here.

"Yeah, dumb-ass," I say, by way of a pep talk.

I let out a big breath, stirring up some of the pine needles in front of my face. There's a decent breeze, chilly fingers reaching in to find me and lifting the corners of my blanket. I tuck it in tighter, curl closer into myself, and pull Davey Beet's hat down to my eyebrows.

"Tomorrow," I tell him. "Tomorrow we're going to get shit done."

DAY ELEVEN

It's raining again in the morning, but I said I was going to move today. So I will.

I get soaked just crawling out from under the pine, cold drops leaving chilly rivulets on my skin. I tie the blanket at my neck, but I can't do much to keep it closed while I'm walking. It billows out around me, what's left of my shirt barely hanging past my bra. My jeans are wet up to my knees in under a minute, Davey's hat a soggy mess.

I put my sling on, tucking my bad foot behind me and ignoring the complaint from my knee as I do. My good foot has been washed clean by the rain, and it looks soft and naked out in the light, skin already puckering into folds.

"Time to go," I say, as a way of making it final.

I've learned how to make decent time using the walking stick as a crutch, and I set a good pace at the outset, spotting the best place to plant the stick, swing myself forward, and bring down my good foot. It's exhausting work, both physically and mentally. I get a headache fast today, probably half from wearing out my eyes in the rain and half from being hungry again.

I'm back to being in pain, and part of the reason I didn't just wrap up in my moldy blanket and stay under that pine until people or coyotes found my body was because if that happens then I killed a momma possum for no good reason. If I decide to just sit down and die, then all she did was give me a few more days to hurt in, and I don't think that would square with her, or her babies. I'm determined to save my own life, not because it's worth living but because I don't want to disappoint a dead possum.

It's a dumb thing to think, but it makes me laugh, distracting me from the gathering storm right up until it almost kills me. Thunder breaks overhead, so close that I jump, walking stick going out from underneath me as I stumble forward, landing on my hands and knees.

A tree goes down behind me, whacking branches left and right from its neighbors and hitting the forest floor with a shudder that I feel in my bones. It falls right where I had been, trunk only about as wide as my waist but that's more than enough to knock the life right out of me—or worse, not kill me outright but leave me crushed, trapped and dying with days to go.

"Fuck," I say.

A fresh gust of wind pushes through the woods, blowing everything that doesn't have roots in front of it. Leaves fly past, a stick goes tumbling by to whip my face, and another crash fills the woods. It vibrates right up into my fingers, the very ground shuddering because something big just met its end.

"Fuck," I say again.

This is a real storm, not a bit of rain or a gust of wind that'll blow over in a minute or so. There's something menacing in the air, everything tinted with a faint pink that means trouble, and I was too busy thinking about a dead possum to notice it.

I get onto my good foot, easing the walking stick back under my armpit. The rain falls so heavy I can't even see individual drops, just a wall of water coming down from the sky that changes directions every time the wind gusts, but always seems to be landing in my face anyway.

Lightning breaks nearby close enough that I can smell it, sharp and acrid. That gets me moving again, but I don't know what toward. I can't go low because all the water will be rising, streams good for me to drink from just minutes before now wanting to pull me into them. I can't climb either, because lightning always hits high spots, and standing near a big tree is like asking to be electrocuted—or crushed. The wind rises once more, strong enough to push me forward.

I stop where I'm at to wipe the rain out of my eyes, a futile effort. I've got no cover and no way to know which way safety lies, or any chance of making it there if I did. Everything is against me: the wind, the rain, the trees themselves. The nature I've respected all my life has no interest in showing me the same.

"So fuck it," I say, quiet.

I get another push from behind for that, the wind not happy with me.

"No, really," I say, tossing my walking stick out into the trees, no longer a tool but one of a million sticks. I'm done trying and being careful and doing my best. If a tree is going to fall on me I'm going to be standing up straight when it happens.

"Fuck. It," I say again, yanking my foot out of the sling.

And then I run.

I am a wild woman.

I run through the rain, though it spits hard enough

to leave welts on my skin, my blanket flying behind me. There is a snap to my left and I change direction suddenly, like prey evading a predator. The tree falls, splinters flying to slice my face. I do not care. I am still running, reveling in the speed, rejoicing in the freedom, moving fast toward nothing.

I do not know if I am panicking or if this is the most sane I have ever been. Have I finally lost it, or did I only realize that there is no hope, and to run through a storm is better than to die curled under a tree? There is something freeing in giving up and accepting that I am going to die out here. If the woods will have me, then first I will drink all it has to offer, a child once again, uncaring as to how I look or what others may think. I am utterly alone, untethered.

My balance is off, the severed part of my foot no longer there to hold me, but I learn the new steps quickly, ignoring the pain. My lungs burn, rain flies in my face, my legs ache and my foot is a savaged piece of meat, but I press on. I'm punishing my body, angry at it for not being strong enough to get me through, for succumbing to weakness and starvation and wounding. It is only a husk of the real me, deep inside, the Ashley who isn't done living but whose body can't keep going.

"Fuck you," I say again, this one a breathless gasp, the words tasting like bile and dandelion greens as what little I have in my stomach surges upward. There is nothing left in me, not food or energy, only willpower. Even my own body has turned on me, and all I can do is force it forward, a breaking-down vehicle for the Ashley trapped inside.

The storm has passed, the sun breaking through the clouds, but still I run, simultaneously panicked and invincible. The animals might not know to be afraid of me, but they are learning. There's movement in the brush to my left when I spook something. I spin, whiskey bottle arcing out from where it's tied to my belt loop to crash against a tree, glass shattering in a thousand pieces as the sun illuminates the shards, airborne.

I pitch backward, arms spinning, my bad foot searching for purchase and unable to find it. There's a moment when gravity doesn't have me yet and I can see clearly through a break in the canopy where a jet leaves a white tail behind it. Civilization is only miles away, but straight up, unreachable.

Then I'm falling.

On the way down the ridge I . . .

Crack my head on a tree, losing a chunk of hair.

Slice my leg on the broken bottle mouth still hanging from my jeans.

Break a rib.

Sprain my wrist.

Lose two teeth.

And the whole time, I am laughing.

I land on my stomach, any air I had left knocked out of me, along with what little food was inside my stomach. It all comes up, dandelion shreds, stomach acid, creek water, and a few worms. Everything I have hurts, but none of it seems to matter as I pull myself into a sitting position and lean against a tree, tasting blood. I left hair and teeth and I'm sure more than a little skin on the ridge above me, a little something to leave behind before nature gets the rest.

"Shit," I say, and spit out some dirt, along with red-tinted spit.

I'm done in, my fit having taken everything I had left. I'm not dead yet, but I might as well be, because my limbs are so heavy I can't move, and my eyelids are starting to feel the same. I might've knocked myself silly on the way down, I realize. Which could be part of why I'm not so worried about dying now, whether it's here or a few yards away after I find it in me to crawl for a little bit.

Crawl toward nothing. Nothing and no one.

I look ahead anyway, pure curiosity making me wonder if there's anything better ahead that I can die next to. The mist clears as a little breeze pushes through.

And I spot a tent.

* * *

It says a lot that the first thing I do when I see a sign of another human being is hide. I've been too long in the woods, too long on my own. I should be running toward that tent screaming for help, but my first instinct is to hunker down. I've been among the animals so long that I'm thinking like one, sure that anything that's not me is out to hurt and the best thing to do is wait and watch and not give myself away.

That's what I do, peering through some wild blackberries that are just showing their leaves, though their thorns make themselves known right away. I've drawn blood on my forearms twice before I'm settled among them, my legs not able to hold a crouch for long. I sit and watch, but nothing is happening, and soon my brain is calming from the scare and I notice that the pegs holding the tent down are brown with rust, the edges of each tent corner frayed and weathered.

Then I see the backpack resting against the tree. I didn't spot it right away because it's faded and worn, with a colony of mushrooms sprouting from one side. I pull myself up, ignoring the thorns that try to hold me back as I go, like they don't want me to have to suffer this one last thing.

But it's too late. I already know.

I knew when I took a deep breath and a good look at

that tent. I knew when I saw the rotted backpack, one that I'd kept my eyes on as I trotted through the woods, smaller feet trying to keep up with the pair in front of me. I knew before I walked up to it. Knew before I flipped it over, just to be sure. There on the back, embroidered in a proud font his mom had picked out and painstakingly sewed onto the thing her son loved best, it read:

PROPERTY OF DAVEY BEET

I'm screwing up the courage to unzip the tent.

I've done a lot of hard things in my life, always putting on a brave face and pulling on my own bootstraps. I said goodbye to my momma, bought groceries with food stamps while keeping my upper lip stiff, lived with a garbage bag for a window instead of glass for a few years. I've been left behind, never having the chance or the inclination to do the leaving.

Now I'm standing here with half a foot and a swelling wrist, a broken rib, and a spreading bloodstain on my jeans from where the whiskey bottle got me, so surely I can gather the courage to undo a zipper. I take a deep breath—which hurts like a bitch because of the rib—and I just do it. It's a simple action, one that doesn't reveal anything I didn't already know.

Davey died curled into a ball, either from hunger or pain or the realization that no one was coming for him and the only person he could get close to was himself. His knees are up to his chest, bones poking through the worn cargoes he always hiked in, his skull resting against his kneecaps.

I wonder if he missed his hat as he was dying, if it could have been a pillow or a reminder of his mom or something to hold on to and make him push through and get back home. I crawl in beside him and tear it off my head to put it on his, pulling it down over his ears—which are still there, wrinkled and small, but there.

"I'm so sorry, Davey," I say, my voice breaking as I cry.

I'm crying for him and for me, because wild woman or not, I know that Davey Beet had the best chance of anyone to make it out of this place alone, and he didn't. I didn't think I had much of a shot left when I lost my head, so adding all the hurts from rolling down the ridge didn't do me any favors.

But it led me to him, so I can't exactly wish it back.

"I've been looking for you," I tell Davey, settling in beside him.

And it's true. Maybe not in the beginning, but certainly once my thoughts started going to this boy, like there was something connecting us, something that drew me to his hat, then to where he carved his name, and now here, to Davey himself. Like maybe all the thoughts I spent on him went up in the air and got twirled around together, and maybe I wouldn't be kidding myself too hard to suppose he was thinking about me every now and then, too. And maybe those thoughts made something like cordage between him and me, enough to bring me here, now.

"Is that what happened, Davey?" I ask.

I end up asking Davey a lot of things, about whether he thought I've done a good job in the woods up to now, and if he thinks I should feel bad about killing that possum, or if it was the right thing to do. Because Davey Beet would know what was the right thing, and he'd do it, every time.

I want him to know that I listened to everything he ever told me, that I made a fireboard and ate the right plants, that I used my own hair to make cordage, and built a shelter out of pine boughs. I want him to know that all those things added up so that I wouldn't die out there, and led me here.

To the place where I wanted to be.

So I lie down in the only bed I'll ever share with Davey Beet, and I close my eyes.

DAY TWELVE

I wake to the sound of rain pattering on the roof of the tent.

There's a leak in one corner, so I've got cold rainwater dripping down my neck when I notice a picture stuck above me in the supporting poles. I can only assume this is the girl that broke Davey's heart, and I want to cry just looking at her.

She's everything I'm not. Blond. Well dressed. Legs that look like they never grew hair in the first place, let alone need shaving. The kind of tan that doesn't have white lines from a sports bra. She's got on makeup and it doesn't look funny on her like it does me. I always hold my face wrong, worried about smearing lipstick or weirded out by the fact that I can see my own eyelashes.

Meredith stopped giving me makeovers because she said I always look like I'm about to either sneeze or vomit.

Apparently neither one of those looks attracts boys.

But the girl looking down on me right now didn't have that problem. She looks like she knows how to talk to boys and what to do with them later too. And while they don't look a thing alike, I feel my fists curling up just looking at this girl because whatever it is she has, Natalie does too, and it makes boys like Duke and Davey act like fools, leaving girls like me to sit by themselves and wonder what we're lacking.

"Goddammit, Davey," I say, shoving him in the back. There's not much left of him, so he goes over a little bit, arm sliding down to slip over his face, like he's hiding from that girl even now.

"What was it about her, huh?" I yell at him. I've been spinning this great idea about how we were supposed to be together, cheated by time and chance, and here Davey died staring up at this girl who's just so damned . . . *city*.

Maybe he never gave me a second thought. Maybe I imagined that lingering glance at the gas station. Maybe I was always only just a kid to him, a little sister tagging along that he could teach things to. And maybe it's my own fault for making Davey Beet into a hero in my mind, the perfect guy for me that maybe didn't ever exist in the first place.

Or maybe he did think I did a good job growing up. Maybe he was coming out here to get this girl out of his system for good. Maybe he looked up at his ceiling once or twice and thought about me, or at least wondered what I was up to.

Maybe this and maybe that. I'll never know for sure because the only person who can answer my questions is dead next to me, the closest we've ever been, years too late.

"Shithole," I say, because it's the only thing I can think of and I've already told everything from the sky to the ground to fuck off. It stops raining, the drops tapering down to bits of nothing so that I can probably get moving again.

I sit up at the thought, gasping at the pain in my rib but already halfway up so I finish the job. I laid down last night thinking that if Davey Beet couldn't make it, then I sure as hell won't. But after a good sleep and a temper tantrum, I'd like to prove otherwise.

I think it's that girl, to be honest.

Some people said Davey Beet came in here never meaning to leave, that she had broken him to a point that he couldn't come back from. What if they're saying the same about me? What if Duke's busted nose and Natalie's snide little smile make everyone think Ashley Hawkins would rather be dead than without him?

"Fuck that," I tell Davey. "I'd rather be alive with half a foot and a busted rib and a sprained wrist and covered in my own blood and mostly naked and wearing a moldy blanket, but a-fucking-live."

"Damn straight," I say back to myself, because I think that's what Davey would've said.

"And single," I add.

And that's how I end up taking Davey Beet's hat back.

Because I need it more than he does.

I take some other things, too.

Davey's shoes are way too big, something I find out after going through the process of taking them off him. His pack has a few things that are helpful to me; a Swiss Army knife, a canteen, and a tarp. I recognize the first two. I've held them before, Davey showing me how to always cut away from myself with the knife, my eyes lingering a little too long on his mouth when he took a drink from the canteen. They're not mine now, not really. They're Davey's, on loan to me for as long as it takes.

I think about staying one more night. It'd be a few more hours with something between me and the sky, a little bit more time with someone that means something to me, even if I'm not quite clear on exactly what that is. But in the end, I decide that the tent can't do anything for me that the tarp won't, and what's left lying in there isn't Davey. Not really. Davey's gone and was never mine to begin with, so I might as well put on a hard face and point it in whatever direction feels best and get on with it.

I do two things before I go.

I found a bandanna deep in Davey's backpack, one that was bought new and still had creases from being folded in a perfect square, though it's spent two years wedged between a camp frying pan and an extra pair of jeans. I tie a stone in the corner for weight and toss it wildly five times before it snags on a branch about twenty feet up, a bright blistering red among all the green. The breeze catches it and it unfolds, factory-pressed corners finally loosed.

I ease myself down with shaky arms and give Davey's pack a critical look. The straps are so rotted I don't think it'll last more than a few miles and I'm so weak I doubt I can carry more than what I already have. The last thing I do is zip the tent again, making sure Davey won't be bothered any more. My hand lingers on the closed flap, like maybe I should say something that isn't swearing.

"I'll come back for you, Davey Beet," I tell him.

And even though he's past saving, I imagine there's some comfort in those words.

* * *

I used to pretend to be asleep, just so Dad would carry me.

When I was a kid I thought we spent a lot of time in the woods because we were outdoorsy people, but as I got older I realized that the woods are also free—and so was a lot of the other stuff we did for fun. Other kids would go bowling or to the zoo, but Dad always offered up options like the library, the park, or fishing with worms we dug up ourselves, never taking the easy way of buying some at the gas station.

We walked everywhere too, me following Dad with my pole leaned back against my shoulder, worn-out sneakers pounding along the cracked sidewalk as I waved at my friends hanging out at the pool, bodies warm in the sun, their summer passes allowing them that luxury. And if I'm being honest, I wasn't all that jealous. Because those kids at the pool and the bowling alley, they didn't have their dads with them, holding their hands when they crossed the street or showing them how to bait a hook. I never needed anything more and didn't really start wanting it until I got older.

Dad's friends were the same kind of people, happy to drink cheap beer and sit in aluminum folding chairs on the front lawn while us kids chased each other, the littler ones wearing clothes the bigger ones had grown out of. Our games were made of mud and sticks, rocks and dirt. And we were happy.

I'd nod off, content in someone else's house, a scratched DVD playing while my sweaty cheek stuck to a cheap leather couch, a bowl of suckers someone had nicked from the dentist's office sitting on the floor.

The adults always followed a pattern; soft chuckles as they warmed up that led into bursts of loud laughter as the beer made jokes funnier, the speaker more clever. People would show up and the noise would swell, becoming a wall of sound with no individual words, just spikes of hilarity. That would fade, sharp slaps of the screen door opening and closing as people came and went, the population of the kids dwindling as their parents left.

The host always offered to let the remaining ones stay, have their parents come get them in the morning. That was my cue to fake sleep, head tipped back, hands open and loose, encouraging a bit of drool to slip out of my mouth. I knew Dad would never leave me; he always felt better if I was home with him, what was left of our family safe under one roof, even if it did leak. So I'd wait for him to come, struggling to keep my body in an approximation of sleep when I was so tense, hoping he'd fall for it.

Maybe he knew I was faking it every time, or maybe he'd had so many beers I didn't need to try so hard. Either way, it didn't matter. Dad always scooped me up, strong arms tight around me, beard scratching against my cheeks, still sticky with sucker, popcorn butter, or the last swig of juice that I'd missed my mouth with. And even though I'd stayed awake all night waiting for the moment for Dad to come and get me, I always fell asleep on the walk back home, safe and happy with him.

I left Davey behind with a few hours of sunlight left, afraid to stay much longer or else I might lose the determination to leave. His tent is a mile or so behind me when I stop to examine my foot. I did a number on it when I decided to go crazy in the storm, losing my plastic bag as I ran. The scab that had started to form was torn off at some point, and I managed to nick off a little more of exposed bone in the process. But Davey had some antibiotic creams and extra socks rolled together in his pack, which I lifted from him along with the knife and canteen.

Now that I'm far enough away from the tent that I won't consider lingering I find some running water to check out the slice in my leg, which doesn't look good but won't kill me. I clean my foot too, wincing at the coldness of it. I'm still swollen, still hurting, still nowhere near what I'd call healing. The antibiotic cream is a startling white out here among all this dirt. It feels good going on, a hell of a lot better than the sock, even though I ease it on over the wound.

I sling my foot back and test my weight against a new walking stick I found. The only good thing I have to say about it is that it rubs in all new places as I go, leaving the old ones alone. I take inventory, touching each thing as I do. My fireboard and broken whiskey bottle top I couldn't quite part with dangle from my belt loops, flint and Davey's knife in my pocket, a reassuring bulge, parts of my dead foot still hanging in a sandwich bag. His tarp is folded neatly and tucked into the back of my jeans, filling the empty space my shrinking body has left behind. My blanket is tied around my throat, what's left of Davey's hat clinging around my ears.

I'm moving.

But Lord do I wish there was someone to carry me.

DAY THIRTEEN

The next day dawns warm, humidity plastering my hair to my head and sending rivulets of sweat to trickle down my side before I've even limped from my camp to the creek. I stick my whole head in the water, running my fingers through my hair as I do, the closest thing to clean that I can get. My fingers find something and I pop back up for air, creek water running down all sides of me, pooling in my bra. I keep my thumb and forefinger pinched tight as I sit down on the bank to give a good tug, and the tick comes off in my palm.

It's fat like a grape, skin mottled and stretched as it's fed on me for I don't know how long. A while, guessing by the size of it. It's so full of my blood that its body has covered its legs, so that it's only a hungry head and a too-full belly. It's warm against my hand, like a cooked bean, and I pop it in my mouth, crunching down. My own blood fills my mouth, slick and coppery.

I slip down onto my stomach, ribs pressing hard against sharp stones. Davey Beet could pull fish out of a creek like reaching into a cooler for a beer, nothing to it. He'd tried to teach me, but I'd never been able, only coming close once when I managed to knock a small-mouth onto the bank and it had flipped and flopped between us, making me screech and him laugh until the poor thing found the water again and left us behind with a splash.

I couldn't do it then, but I wasn't dying then, either. And today there's no chance of me being distracted by Davey's freckled arm close to mine, or how his hands glided smooth and slow under the water. I know the fate of those hands, and how that arm looks now. The only place my mind wanders as I wait for an unwary fish to pass by is if I'm going to end up looking the same, and how soon.

Nevertheless, I'm too anxious with the first two fish that pass under my hand, wiggling my fingers along with the current. I twitch the wrong way at the wrong moment and they split, sensing that something's off. It's not until I'm warm from the sun, sweat running down in between my shoulder blades and half-asleep myself that I feel one brush up against my palm.

I move fast, clenching my fist tight and jerking my arm out of the water. I'm not smooth like Davey, pulling it up and out with confidence. It's more like I just toss a whole bunch of water along with a fish up onto the shore, but the result is the same—a white-bellied trout tossing on the rocks, gills opening and closing as it drowns in air.

I've got a knife and a piece of tin and I can sure as hell make a fire, but all those thoughts are human and logical, and they pass like a quick rainstorm. A larger part of my mind is desperate and half-wild, fishing like a bear, and eating like one too.

The fish is small and goes down easy; its tail flapping against the roof of my mouth for a brief second before it's gone. I sit on the bank, feel it make a cold journey, still twitching, down into my stomach. It rests there for a moment as if confused, then stages a last revolt, panicked and flailing in my gut.

It's too much for my shriveled stomach and I vomit, bending forward onto hands and knees as the fish makes its way back up my throat, accompanied by a handful of fern fronds. It breaks out from between my teeth and lands in the stream, bile-coated and shocked, but alive. I blink and it's gone, and I'd swear the whole thing never happened in the first place if it weren't for the scales coating my lips.

I lick them off, take a drink of cold water, and keep moving.

At camp they told us the story of Jonah and the whale, how God asked Jonah to do something (I forget what) and Jonah didn't like it, so he got on a boat and went the opposite direction of where he was supposed to. There was a storm, the boat sank, and Jonah would have died except for a whale swallowed him, and he lived in that thing's belly for three days, praying for deliverance, and the whale burped him back out. Then Jonah went and did the thing he was supposed to do in the first place, feeling properly chastised.

I don't know if that fellow I ate was saying a fish version of a prayer as it flipped and flopped in my belly, but the result was the same. It came back up and maybe right now it's going to go do something it's supposed to do with its life, delivered from certain death. I'm contemplating whether fish have a purpose other than making more fish when I get spots in my vision and have to sit down.

I haven't moved far from where I slept, maybe only half a mile. I've got creek water and bile in my stomach, but that's about it. It sloshes as I go from sitting to lying, my head fuzzy and my eyes still far from clear.

At camp they told us that Jonah's story was about second chances, that God wanted something out of him and Jonah went against that but had the opportunity to try again. I don't know if I'm going to get a chance to fix things I've done wrong, but I know what they are now, if nothing else.

I need to tell Duke I'm sorry I broke his nose, because I am. He sure as hell deserved it, but that doesn't mean I don't feel bad about it. I used my hands to break his bones and shed his blood, and that's as wrong as what he did with his.

I need to tell Dad I don't mind the trailer so much, that living there with him has been the best thing in my life. He's the only person that's been true to me through thick and thin, and I'll be the first to admit that I haven't exactly made it easy for him. He's stuck it out and always made being a dad the most important thing in his life—more important than finding a girl-friend or hanging out with his buddies. He's never left me behind, and I'm not sure I can say the same.

I need to tell Laney Uncapher that she would've beaten me on that cross-country course if I hadn't busted her eye, and that she shouldn't give up running just 'cause she's a mom now because it's the things you don't do that you regret. She should know that.

I need to tell Meredith that we don't have a damn thing in common but I love her right down to her bones and that she can put makeup on me anytime and I'll try to hold my face right and maybe I'll take her hiking without giving her shit every five minutes. I need to fix the things that have gone wrong between us, because when you're Ashley Hawkins you only have so many friends and you need to put the work into keeping them.

I need to tell Kavita she's the strongest person I've ever known, stronger even than me because she does it without hurting anyone. She puts up with all the comments about her skin and the boys asking what color her nipples are and she just holds her head up like they aren't anything to her, when I'd be busting skulls. I never did bust a skull, or even open my mouth when other people threw shit at her. I just assumed she could take care of herself and didn't want the help, same as I would. But maybe she could've used a word from me, and I should've said it.

I need to tell my momma I did need her after all, and maybe I could've tried harder to sit still while she brushed out my hair or let her braid it once in a while.

There's a lot of things I need to do, but I am so tired.

DAY FOURTEEN

I sleep for an entire day and night under a tree, at one point feeling the soft paws of a squirrel on my face, curious. I wonder if it's the same one from the beginning of all this, and if he's been following me all along, wanting to know how it would end.

I'm wondering about that, too.

DAY FIFTEEN

I get back up, and it's because of Coach.

At the end of the district championship race my sophomore year I collapsed after the finish line and couldn't
get back up. Somebody ran to get Coach, and he knelt
in front of me and said, "You can't go home unless you
get on the bus, and I'm not carrying you."

So I got up.

This might be one fucked-up 5K—and a hell of a
lot longer—but the idea is the same. You aim for the
finish line: that's your goal. But beyond that, you get to
go home, and you only get to do that if you're moving.

I'm hitting a finish line today. I don't know which
one, or what home is behind it—the one with my dad
in it, or the one that everyone at Camp Little Fish kept

telling me about—but I'm fucking going. And it's today.

I unsling my foot because I'll make better time without crutching along. Davey's sock is filthy and soaked through from an afternoon rain by midday, but it doesn't seem to matter much anymore. I can't remember what I own that is mine and what is Davey's, or which one of us is who either. Maybe I am still back in that tent, and the fish and my long sleep under the tree and everything happening now is just a fever dream as I slip away, dying next to a boy I admired maybe a little too much.

Maybe it's Davey walking through the woods now, my flesh on his bones, making his way back to a family that loved him and a future brighter than mine. Maybe I came out here to give something back and he's going to break out of the trees and tell everyone that Ass-kicker Ashley showed up to save him, and her life is in him now and we are finally one.

"That's fucking weird," I say, which seems to have some effect on bringing me into the present. That, and the sharp end of a stick that pokes into the soft ridge of my good foot, bringing a bright flash of reality that snaps my mind back from where it had been roaming.

I sit and pull my foot up to see what kind of damage I've done to myself this time. There's a decent scrape but no puncture. I lift the corner of my blanket and wipe the sweat from my face. I've been tempted to dump it once or twice, but I only own so many things at this point, and I admit to being attached to my moldy meth blanket.

I'm staring at the scrape, noticing how it's shaped almost like the scar on my knee from where a neighbor laid down his dirt bike when I was seven and riding on the back, when I realize the rain doesn't sound right. It's falling in small drops, fat lazy ones like winter flies, but that's not what has my attention. Somewhere nearby, they're pinging off metal.

I don't know what to expect when I follow the noise, my path crooked and shaky. I come to a break in the trees and there in the middle of the woods is an oil well. It's the only sign of humans that I've seen in weeks, so I sit down and take it in.

It's a dead thing, the head no longer rising and falling the way it was made to. Normally I'd be pissed at seeing this thing left out here to rust and bleed out into the ground. But right now it's a slice of civilization, proof that someone, at some point, stood here. It's got a bit of its own beauty to me for that reason, and I call it downright gorgeous when I get to its best quality.

A ladder.

I don't expect to see anything much when I start climbing, other than a good view, since it's built on the top of a ridge and everything around it is nicely cleared. I'll probably see more trees and maybe an eagle if I'm lucky, although I wouldn't be surprised if what I get instead are buzzards that have already started circling.

I'm halfway up and both my feet are giving me hell and I'm feeling woozy from the height, but I keep going, because the only thing at the bottom is the ground and I've been hanging out there long enough. When I get to the top I get what I expected, a sea of green, endless trees and rolling hills, their beauty undeniable even though it probably spells death for me. I let out a sigh, determined to enjoy the view if nothing else, when a gust of wind blows away some low-hanging mist and in the distance there's something new.

Electric lines.

I have a destination.

For the first time in forever I'm pointing toward something and not going blindly, which gives me hope. It's not something I can put in my stomach or that adds speed to my steps, but it does give me the strength to take one more, and then another. I'm pointed in the right direction and making time when it starts to sprinkle, small drops hitting my face and trickling down my neck. I don't bother wiping them away, intent on saving every bit of energy I have for one thing and one thing only.

I'm so focused on my steps that my feet are all I'm looking at, willpower being the only thing I've got left in me. I move one and then the other, the simple repetition of socked foot, then naked foot, being one that might—just might—save my life. I'm singing "The Bear Went Over the Mountain" again, moving my feet in time with the song, counting how many verses it takes me to get to where I'm headed.

I'm twenty-three repetitions in when I break out of the trees, although I almost pass right underneath the electric lines without noticing them because all my concentration is pointed downward. It's their buzzing that finally gets my attention.

Electric lines cut through the woods like scars, the trees cleared out for a ways on either side, the sloping wires reaching across and over valleys with huge spires between them. The one I'm under now looks something like the Eiffel Tower, or at least the closest I'm ever going to get to it. I stare up at it, losing my balance and going over in a pile of musty blanket and stale sweat. I'm pissed at myself for falling when all I've got to do is follow this clean cut across the forest that'll lead me back to civilization.

I happen to fall the right way so that I'm facing a utility station, far enough out that I can just see it, and little dots of orange moving around it. I sit up, black spots joining those bright splashes of color that I realize are people, and dear God, I cannot faint right now.

"Get up," I say, either in my head or out loud. I don't know enough to tell the two apart anymore. I drag myself to my feet and push what's left of Davey Beet's hat off my forehead, squinting into the distance.

There's a service road and a white truck, two people wearing the bright orange that I always cursed for breaking up my view in the past, but right now is a beacon for me to run toward with everything I've got left—which isn't much.

"Jesus Christ, get up, Ashley," I say. "They're right there."

Except I can't. My knees have finally given out, every muscle I've got collapsed. I finished the race, but the bus is leaving and Coach won't carry me and I'm not going to make it. I'm going to die leaning against this electric pole, or right at the finish line. I don't know which is which anymore, like the cans of tomato soup lined up in the middle of a blizzard keeping me warm while I died in the snow. Dad came out to get me that time, but there's no one here.

This is my call, and I make the decision.

I am running, and I am screaming. I don't have words or anything close to language anymore, just a plea, a wild sound that I hope carries as I run toward them, willing them to see me, to hear me.

I am Ashley Hawkins and I am not dead yet, dammit, and my blanket streaks behind me, my fireboard and broken whiskey top whipping against my legs, Davey Beet's canteen snug against my hip and his hat slipping down to my eyebrows as the rain keeps falling and it runs into my mouth, tinting my screams with the taste of a storm.

They hear me. They see me.

They are running toward me, cutting the distance that I have to cover, and I'm so grateful I could cry, but there's no tears left inside. My legs burn, and darkness is spotting my vision and my feet are the heaviest they have ever been, but I keep going, denying the pain, focusing on the buzz of the electrical wires above me and the straight line they make between me and other human beings.

We meet under the shadow of a spire, the sun breaking out for a moment to show me these people, a woman with a blond ponytail and a man with a red beard. I collapse in front of them, trying to find words to say everything that needs to be said, to explain the woods and the possum, the bag at my side that holds what's left of my foot, Davey Beet's bloody sock and how deeply my eyes are sunk into my head.

What I say is:

"My name is Ashley Hawkins, and I need help."

PART THREE

AFTER
I
WAS
FOUND

The man calls 911 as the woman walks by my side, back to the truck, telling me to watch out for things like dips in the ground and the little mound where the extra stone got dumped in a pile when they were putting in the service road. Normally I might be amused at anyone being worried that some gravel might break me in half, but then again, I have no idea what I look like now. And to be honest, it might.

She keeps talking, and I realize that she's waiting for me to say something more than my name, but I don't know what else matters. Instead I sit in the grass near the truck, forearms resting on my knees. Then I see the license plate.

"Hey," I interrupt the woman, who is digging in the

truck for something. She turns around, a brown bag in her hand.

"Am I in Georgia or are you in Tennessee?"

Her eyebrows come together, and I know I need to try again, find better words for what I'm asking. It made sense to me in my head, and since I'm the only person I've been talking to for a while, I thought it would do the trick.

"Where am I?"

"Georgia," she answers, handing me a water bottle. "We both are."

"Huh," I say, and try to twist the cap off. It won't move. She reaches for it and cracks the seal, then hands it back to me.

"I got it started for you," I tell her, and she laughs. It's a wonderful sound, strong and full, without the edge mine has started to develop.

"So I walked right out of Tennessee?" I ask, taking a drink of water.

"If that's where you started, then yes," she says.

The water hits my stomach, and I flinch. I don't want to puke in front of this woman, don't want her to know that it doesn't taste like real water because there's no dirt trailing on my tongue, or an aftertaste of fish. Everything about it, from the clarity of the plastic to the ridged cap in my hand is off, and I feel an edge of panic when I realize I'm going to have to get into the truck eventually.

"What's your name?" I ask the woman, taking another experimental sip.

"Tammy," she says, and holds out her hand for me to shake. I do, noticing how thin my fingers are inside of hers, a scrape the shape of Florida across the top of my left hand, and the filth under my fingernails.

"What's this?" Tammy asks, reaching out to touch Davey Beet's hat. I shy away, dumping some of the water in my lap. I can stand to have someone touch me, but Davey's stuff is another story and not one I'll tell to just anybody.

"It's a hat," I say.

Tammy nods and slowly sits down next to me, propping her elbows on her legs like I do. I pull my blanket closer around me, covering my fireboard and whiskey bottle, like I'm afraid she might try to take them away.

"She's from *where*?" the guy's voice cuts across the space between us, the phone conversation clearly going places he hadn't expected. Just like I did.

"Hungry?" Tammy asks, reaching into her lunch to pull out a bologna-and-cheese sandwich.

The truth is I'm not. I'm too far gone to consider being hungry. But the sight of the sandwich carefully tucked into a bag with a fold-over top makes me think of Meredith, and all the supposedly extra bologna-and-cheese sandwiches she'd brought to school for years, even though I knew damn well she hated bologna.

I start to cry.

The woman puts her arm around me, and I lean into her, smelling the clean scent of her shampoo and the simple warmth of her and how solid she is. I take a deep breath that feels like it's scraping the back of my throat clear down to the spine, but it can't go deep enough, can't quite reach the place where everything that's happened to me rests.

I've been trying to find words, and I thought I was failing because it'd been so long since I used them, but instead it's because there aren't any that'll work. There's just crying. Crying 'cause I'm happy to be safe, and terrified to see people again. Crying because even though I said my name when I came out of the woods, I don't know if that's who I am anymore. Crying because of Duke and Meredith and Kavita and my dad and how I'll get to see them again, and crying for my momma and Davey Beet because the same isn't true for them. There's lots of reasons to cry, but I've got a mouth and it was made for more than just gasping for air in between sobs.

I stop crying.

And I eat.

* * *

The truck is going impossibly fast.

I made Tammy sit in the middle, next to Paul—who keeps saying, "Tennessee!" over and over again like it's a new state or something. I needed to be near the window, and even though it's still raining I've rolled it down, letting the drops hit my face as we speed toward where the squad is going to meet us once we get down out of the hills and off the service roads. I glance over Tammy's legs at the speedometer, shocked to see it's barely touching forty.

Everything outside is whipping past us so quickly I can't take it in, can't see each tree, touch every leaf. My life has slowed to a point that moving above a crawl feels obscene, and sounds startle me. When Paul started the truck the radio blasted on and Tammy had snapped it off quickly when I yelped, covering my ears with my blanket.

They've both been quiet as we drive, the rain picking up and soaking my arm as I let it drift out the window, feeling the resistance of the breeze against my hand. I look over at Tammy, and she tucks her phone away but not before my own face appears under a news headline.

"You googled me?" I ask.

"Yeah," she says sheepishly, turning her phone over. There's a muted video playing of my dad standing at a podium, the only tie he owns tied all wrong and his dress shirt from Grandpa's funeral too tight across his belly. But I don't think anyone is looking at him, only listening. Faces crumple along with his as he breaks down, and I don't need to hear the words to know that he's asking for someone, please, to bring his little girl back to him.

"I brought myself back," I tell him quietly, my thumb resting against the screen.

There's a long article that I can't read while the truck is moving so fast, the few bites of bologna and cheese that I managed to get down threatening to come back up. I don't want to thank Tammy and Paul by puking on them, so I give her the phone back, aware that she's double-checking the face on the screen and comparing it to the one in front of her. I wonder how hard it is to find a resemblance.

The squad meets us where the service road dumps out on a state route, their lights flashing but sirens off. I pop my truck door and move to get out, but there are suddenly people everywhere, and no one seems to want me to move. A female paramedic scoops me out of the truck like a baby, not even huffing for breath when we make it over to the ambulance, where I'm given a lot of instructions.

Lie back. Relax. Calm down. Breathe normally.

I'm doing all these things, but the medics in the back

with me still have little frowns on their faces as they methodically list everything that has gone wrong with me. They use different words than I would, like *contusion* for *bruise*, *laceration* for *cut* and *malnourished* for *starving*. The male—his lanyard identifies him as Michael— is reeling off these things, and the female is writing quickly across the back of her rubber glove.

The ambulance is rolling and the sirens going. The female medic is still taking notes, flipping her hand over to write on the other side of her glove when Michael eases my sock off.

"Holy fucking shit!" he says, which is pretty much the same words I would use to describe it. I lift my head to look.

"That's nothing," I tell him. "You should've seen it before I took the bad parts off."

"The bad parts?"

"Yeah," I say, reaching for the bag with what's left of my foot inside. "These bits."

I lift it for him to see, and he covers his mouth and looks away real quick, taking a minute to compose himself. Then he lifts my heel gently, turning my foot to see the damage from all angles.

"You took this off?" Michael asks.

"Yeah," I say, lying my head down as the spots threaten again.

"With what?"

"A big chunk of flint." I consider reaching into my pocket to share the sliver I kept with me but decide against it because I don't want it taken away from me.

He whistles low between his teeth and sets my leg back down. "Nice work."

"Thank you," I say, weirdly pleased by the compliment.

"Can you tell me your name?" the other medic asks.

"Ashley," I tell her.

"Okay, Ashley," she says. "I'm Barbara. I'm going to start an IV to keep you hydrated, all right? It's going to make your arm a little cold." She says it apologetically, like it's the worst possible end to my day. There's a pinch and she's done, a needle tucked into the crook of my arm.

"Do you know what day it is?" Barbara asks, and I realize she's trying to decide if I hit my head at some point or not. I definitely did, and I certainly don't know what day it is, but that has nothing to do with having a concussion.

"No," I say.

"Who is the president?" Michael asks, but only gets a snort out of me in response. They exchange a glance, like maybe that answer is kind of common.

"Can you tell us what happened?" Barbara tries, like

she's tossing me an easy one, something I should be able to explain.

"I was lost," I say, the first time I've spoken the word. My voice cracks around it, either because I'm too proud to admit it or because it's so damn terrifying, even now that I'm safe. Because I knew, every time I left my house for the woods, that it could kill me. I just never believed it would try.

"The world is not tame," I tell Barbara, and she nods like maybe she gets it as she wraps a blood-pressure cuff around my arm, then swaps it out for a different one. Judging by the Dora the Explorer sticker on the band I'm guessing it's the one they use on kids, my arm too small for the one made for adults.

"How'd you manage?" Michael asks, eyes still on my foot.

"There was no one else to do it," I tell him. "So I had to."

"No, I mean, like, overall," he says. "Everything."

I only shrug, because the answer is the same.

In the hospital I'm asked a lot of questions I don't know the answers to.

Like who my family doctor is, or if I've had all my immunizations. I tell them we don't usually go to the doctor unless we're bleeding out—we mostly use duct tape when injured and that I assume I have all my shots. Those don't seem to be the answers they were looking for because they give me a whole bunch more shots, including one for tetanus even though I tell them I'm pretty sure I'm up-to-date on that because lockjaw is something Dad takes seriously.

Everything is bright here, and overwhelmingly clean. Everyone has smiles on their faces that get bigger when they see me, like I'm the sun peeking out from behind a cloud they never thought would pass. I know I'm like some miracle baby, the girl who was lost and now is found.

The Ashley from before would have been irritated at being wheeled everywhere, insisted on standing and walking because being carted around looks like weakness. But I know exactly how strong I am, and there is beauty in moving smoothly without doing a thing. I slide past doorways and signs with arrows at the end of every hall, kiosks with maps and a star that reads, YOU ARE HERE, popping up every now and then.

I find it reassuring to know exactly where I am.

I'm given a room and a hospital gown, folded up in a neat square like Davey Beet's bandanna was. A nurse asks if I need help changing, or if I want privacy. I opt for the latter, even though you'd think I'd had enough of that by now.

I empty my pockets, setting Davey's knife and my

flint on the little table next to the bed. Then I untie my fireboard and whiskey bottle, lining everything up. My pants ease off without being unbuttoned, my underwear following. I loosen the blanket at my neck, folding it neatly like it's important, even though it's got mold and blood and I don't even know what all on it. My hands go to Davey's hat, which I ease off reluctantly, sitting it with everything else.

What's left of my shirt can fit in my fist, but I have to call in a nurse to help me with the sports bra. I'm too weak to hold my arms and get tangled in it, so she sits me down and does it for me.

"Honey, honey, honey," she says, looking me up and down. It's not embarrassing, because there's not much left to see.

I have to sit on the little shelf inside the shower to get clean, my bad foot perched on a stool outside of the water flow. The woods comes off me in a small pile of sticks and dead leaves and dirt at my feet, all of it washed and sanitized, sucked down the drain along with three more ticks that I find. I feel even thinner once I'm done, like without the woods on me I'm not really me anymore. I'm someone newer, cleaner. Someone a few pounds lighter without all the dirt.

I look in the mirror for the first time and meet this new person.

I'm different; there's no doubt. The angles of my face are sharper, eyes sunk deep. I've got a lighter strip of skin around my forehead where Davey Beet's hat kept the sun off me, and some dirt still stuck in the creases of my neck even though I scrubbed good.

And my hair . . . the nurse had warned me they might have to cut it off, it's such a mess. It's one huge tangle, every strand wound with another, all of it shifting together when I try to lift a single piece. It's cold and heavy, hanging halfway down my back and still dripping when I open the door.

And there's my dad.

"Ash—" He breaks off, like my whole name is too much, too heavy. I move to go over, lose what balance I've got left, but Dad's there, and he catches me. I fall into him, the hard zipper of his jacket jamming right through the hospital gown and into my ribs, because he's lifting me right up off the ground, the tips of my toes barely touching the linoleum. He puts me back down and I sink onto the bed, my rat's nest of hair dripping onto the sheets.

He's unshaven, eyes bloodshot, dark circles all that seems to be left of his face. Dad's probably lost ten pounds himself.

"You look like shit," I tell him.

"You look worse," he says, and sits next to me.

He's so much bigger than I am, so much heavier that the bed sags, and I lean toward him, my head on his shoulder. We just sit there, me soaking in his warmth, his arm resting across my shoulders.

And then I ask him to comb out my hair.

Dad says there's reporters outside.

Apparently, I'm a big deal, and most of the country is celebrating that I've been found. Since 99.9 percent of them didn't know I existed until I was gone, I know better than to be flattered. Dad shows me on his phone where someone started a fund for my medical bills, and while the donation amount is big and the number keeps growing every time he refreshes it, I somehow doubt it's going to be enough.

They move me closer to home, to a hospital in the right state and the right county. A squad takes me, the staff hustling me out a side door so that the reporters don't spot me. I'm something of an odd celebrity, the Girl Who Lived, a hillbilly Harry Potter. Reporters keep wanting to talk to me, and news vans hovered outside the hospital for a few days before they realized that when Ashley Hawkins says *no*, it means *no*.

I know what I look like. I know what I sound like. I might be a hero right now but as soon as I open my mouth there'll be a thousand people saying my accent is cute, and another thousand or so making fun of me for it. I'm not here for them. I didn't live so that people could do impressions of me. I'll keep my words and my voice for those that know me.

Meredith and Kavita are waiting in my room when I get there, Kavita smart enough not to bring flowers or balloons, Meredith emotional enough to bring both. Dad leaves us alone so that we can talk, headed back to the house to bring me some of my own clothes, which I'm finally allowed to wear. My friends settle into chairs by my side, both nervous.

"Hey," they say at the same time, Kavita giving Meredith a soft punch on the arm.

"Guys, it's fine," I say.

"No, I mean—" Kavita says in a rush while Meredith just starts crying.

"Stop," I tell them both, and they do.

"You didn't know," I say, before either can interrupt me. "It wasn't your fault."

Meredith nods like she wants to believe it, but Kavita's frown tells me she's not going to let herself off the hook quite so easily.

"We thought you went home, Ash, I swear," she says.

"I did," I tell her. "I took the long way."

Meredith snorts—something I haven't heard her do since fourth grade—and uses the edge of my bedsheet to wipe her face, which I doubt my nurses would like, but it's so Meredith that I don't care. She's here; she's in front of me; she's my friend, and you take them with the good and the bad—something they've been doing for me for years, and I never thanked them for it.

And I will. I'll say all the things I knew needed to be said when I thought I was dying. But I'll do it when I'm healthy so they can't make light of it and say it's the drugs talking. I'll do it when I can stand on my feet and look them in the eye so that they know how true it is. I'll do it when I'm ready and they are too, when I've got a good handle on who this new Ashley is and she's found the right words.

"So you cut your foot off?" Kavita says.

"Part of it," I correct. "But, yeah. On the floor of a meth lab, with a rock. Then I disinfected with whiskey."

"That's so you," Meredith says. "Some of that hit the news and people on Twitter were calling bullshit, and I was like, whatever, I wouldn't be surprised if she chewed it off with her teeth. So I got in, like, five tweet wars over it."

"Thank you," I tell her, and I mean it.

Kavita rolls her eyes but lets it slide. "I took your pack home for you," she says, efficient as always. "And I charged your phone." She reaches into her back pocket, pulling it out.

"Thanks," I say. I've got thirty-five texts, but I slide it under my pillow for later. "So . . ."

I trail off, unsure of how much they want to hear about the woods, about thinking I would die and deciding that I would and then changing my mind about it. I don't know if Meredith can handle the idea of eating worms and raw fish, and she for sure can't hear the part about the one that swam back up my throat, or about me clubbing a possum to death. Kavita might, and maybe I'll tell her one day, but right now I'm so far from that, here in this clean room, with my friends.

"Omigod." Meredith perks up suddenly. "You don't know because you've been gone, but Kate Fullerton ran over Jake Smalls with her truck at a field party because he said she smelled like week-old period. But it was just his foot, and it was, like, real muddy so he didn't get hurt too bad."

"That's a shame," I say, to which Kavita adds, "Preach."

Meredith keeps going, telling me all the things that went on in my absence, what people said and did, the world that kept going without me in it, stuff that normally I might tell her doesn't matter, that I don't care. But this is my life, and these are the people in it.

And yes, I do care.

* * *

Duke is the last person to show up.

Dad is filling out paperwork so that I can leave tomorrow, but the scratch of his pen falls silent when Duke walks in, and I open my eyes. Dad knows what happened, the story coming out of me while he untangled my hair, so I half expect him to rebreak Duke's nose.

It's still lopsided and a bit yellow right around the bridge, so instead Dad just gives him a once-over and asks me if I want to talk to him. I tell him I do, and Dad leaves, not quite letting the door shut entirely behind him.

"Hey," Duke says, taking a chair next to the bed.

"Hey," I say. He leans forward like he's thinking about taking my hand, so I tuck it under the sheets.

"Ash," he says, eyes down. "I'm so goddamn sorry."

"It's okay," I tell him, and he swallows hard like maybe there's more words stuck in his throat but they're having a hard time coming out. I know how that feels, know what it's like to have all the feelings backed up in there and choking you. I felt like that when I found him in the woods with Natalie.

"I came looking for you," he says after a second, voice small and quiet. "I went all up and down the hills. I did everything I could think of, Ash. But you weren't there."

"No," I agree. "I was long gone and headed the other direction."

It's true in more ways than one, but I know he's got to get it out, so I let Duke tell me about how he found my shoes and socks, the rock where I crushed my foot and the blood there. He tells me about search parties and sniffing dogs and news crews and reporters and people lining up in straight rows and combing the woods for me, Jason yelling himself hoarse. He needs to do it, needs to show me how hard he tried to make up for what went wrong.

"All the reporters, they've been going nuts since you got back," he goes on. "They keep calling me, asking if I've come to see my girlfriend and how you're doing and if you'll talk to them sometime and I just keep telling them, 'Hell, I don't know. Ashley's going to do what she's going to do and you can't make her do different.'"

That's true enough. I can say a lot of things about this boy, but one of them is that he knows me, inside and out.

"Is there anything you want me to tell them?" Duke asks.

"Yeah," I say. "You need to tell them to get their facts straight."

"How's that?" he asks.

"I'm not your girlfriend," I say. "Not anymore."

Duke nods like he's just taking it in, but there's tears in his eyes when he gets up. "All right then," he says, hand on the doorknob. "Feel better, Ashley."

"I already do," I tell him.

When I finally get home there are reporters. The more industrious of the bunch have dug a little and found our address, something that makes me cringe. I'm not ashamed of the overgrown yard or the ripped trampoline, the cinder-block steps and the rusted spots in the metal siding. Maybe once I would've been, but not after I found out what it's like to go without it.

Still, I don't like people poking around outside, waiting for me to hobble out. It's hot enough that we have to open windows, and when we do they call for me from the road, having been warned by Dad not to come into the yard. I ignore them, and eventually they do go away, except for the reporter from the local paper. He's smart enough to know his audience and his people, so he waits until the city folks with their news vans are gone, then he takes a risk and knocks on the door.

I'll talk to him, because I need something in return.

I told Dad about Davey Beet once we were home. Dad just put his head down while I talked about finding Davey's hat, his name on the beech, and finally, Davey himself. Dad never interrupted except to shake his head and say, "Jesus," every now and then.

So when the reporter comes into my room I tell him I need to talk to Davey Beet's parents, and he gets ahold of them for me. They show up the next day, a little bewildered but happy I'm alive, like maybe I put one over on the woods that took their son. We're sitting in the living room—I'm in Dad's broken recliner with my foot up, so it's all awkward when Davey's mom tries to hug me, but I let her. She smells kind of like him, a bit of freshness and a little touch of lemon verbena. When I give her what's left of Davey's hat she just starts crying. Davey's dad puts his hand on her knee, and they sit quietly together, finally knowing.

I tell them about how Davey was in my head the whole time I was out there, how I kept finding little hints of him along the way. I don't tell them about the web of thoughts I'd constructed for myself in the woods, his and mine, pulling us together so that I'd find him. I don't tell them about the picture of that girl, because I don't know if his heart was broken or mine was just bigger, so I could come back home.

I keep those things to myself as I listen to Dad crack open a beer in the kitchen after they've gone. Small noises in a small house.

I'm so goddamn thankful I get to hear them again.

* * *

I get lots of visitors, all of them wearing smiles . . . except for one.

I'd been expecting a call instead, so when a car with the logo of the college I got a cross-country scholarship to pulls into the yard I'm flattered that at least they're coming to talk to me themselves. It's not a representative either, or even the scout. It's the coach. He's a good guy, doesn't waste anybody's time and takes the glass Dad offers him without flinching at the taste of sulfur in the well water. He drinks it down, then leans forward on the couch.

"So, Ashley, I was looking forward to you running for me after high school."

"Except now I can't run," I beat him to the punch, saying it myself so that he knows I already figured out why he's here.

"No," he agrees. "You can't."

He gives Dad a folder outlining my options, says that the university has put together a scholarship for me that will help with tuition if I would still like to attend. But nobody here is a bullshitter, and nobody says maybe I'll be a runner again someday. The truth is I'm still learning how to walk, going to therapy to figure out how to balance right without part of one foot, trying to find a way to hold myself that won't throw my hips out.

I'll be able to again, for sure, maybe even without a limp if I get everything right. But running is in my past, as is the thought of going to college. The scholarship is a nice gesture but an empty one. We don't need help for me to go; we need it to be free.

At Camp Little Fish they liked to tell us that when God closes a door, a window is opened. That never meant much to me in a house where the door always fell off the hinges anyway and most of the windows were stuck shut, but I see things differently now.

So I wait, ready to hear the sound of that window screeching open.

The local paper runs my story.

I didn't hold anything back. I told the reporter about being drunk and going to take a piss (though he said I was "relieving myself"). I told him about beating a possum to death and eating worms and cutting off my foot and popping oxy and pouring whiskey over my wounds and singing "The Bear Went Over the Mountain," and even how I was bleeding from one place when I started out, and a bunch of others by the end.

I tell the ugly truth about all of it, about losing my head and swearing at squirrels, about finding Davey

Beet and lying down to die and waking up alive and being irritated by that fact. I don't hold back, and people seem to like that. So much so that we start getting phone calls.

Dad tells the first few that I've said everything I have to say and then hangs up, but one day he has a conversation I'm half listening to from the living room as I flip through channels, looking for a baseball game, my still-bandaged foot propped on the coffee table.

"Ashley," he says, phone tucked against his shoulder. "I think maybe you should talk to this guy."

It's an outdoors outfitting company, wanting me to be a spokesperson, which is kind of funny considering I survived out there in a sports bra. But there's money involved, and all the equipment I could ever need.

I say yes.

It's a year before I'm able to do what comes next.

I get through my senior year, graduate, and do all the things the old Ashley needed to do, but all my goals have changed. I say everything that needs to be said to Meredith and Kavita, and to Duke, even Laney Uncapher. It doesn't fix everything, and I'm not dumb enough to think it would. Meredith still irritates the shit out of me sometimes, and I can't help the swell of jealousy in my gut when I go to Kavita's races. It matches the one I feel when I hear that Duke is living with Natalie after we graduate, and I can't tell myself that I don't care.

I do, but the world is not tame and neither are people, or how I feel about them.

It's spring and I'm standing at a trailhead, a pack of the best gear that exists on my back and a special pair of shoes the company made just for me, balanced out so that I feel like I've got a whole foot. I've got a handheld GPS and even a personal tracker that Dad insisted on so that I can send a message if I need help. There's a pack of pens and an empty notebook in there too, to take notes for a writer who wants to tell my story. When she contacted me, I told her my story wasn't over yet.

So here I am, listening to the sound of Dad's truck fading away as he leaves. I've got Davey Beet's hat on my head and my old blanket too, though his mom remade the top of his hat and gave it back to me and insisted on washing the mold out of my meth blanket. They're my same old things, just better versions for this part of the trip, and I guess that only makes sense, since it's true of me too.

I'm going to find Davey Beet. I'm going to bring home the boy who showed me how to survive. Then I'm going to live every day remembering that's what we're all doing, each in our own way.

But nobody wants to do it alone.

I hike up my pack and square my shoulders.

And I go back into the woods.

ACKNOWLEDGMENTS

This is my ninth published book, and writing the acknowledgments is a lesson on how often you rely on the same people. Eternal thanks to my agent, Adriann Ranta Zurhellen, who rolls with everything I throw at her and reins me in when necessary. She's a keeper. This is my fifth book with my editor Ben Rosenthal, who I truly appreciate—not many authors have the freedom to experiment across genres. Ben takes chances with me, and I may revel in that a bit.

Cover designer Erin Fitzsimmons continues to astonish and amaze. She's covered all my books and I'm constantly hearing from readers, fans, and publishing insiders that I get the best covers. That's because I have the best cover designer.

The entire team at Katherine Tegen is a treasure, and I truly believe there is no better imprint to be with. There's support, communication, and thoughtful exchange—and that's not always the case in this industry.

As always, my friends and fellow writers are indispensable. Thank you to Kate Karyus Quinn, Demitria Lunetta, Natalie D. Richards, and R.C. Lewis, for just being you, and letting me be me . . . which I totally know is sometimes a lot.

Lastly, a big thanks to my people—librarians, educators, and readers. This is my fan base. It's because of you continuing to pick up my books and recommend them to friends that I have the opportunity to be a writer. Without readers, writers don't exist.

And—honestly, go ahead and recommend my books to your enemies, too.